To: Lucille -
With love -
Katie Carothers

White Trash

A Novel
by

Katie Carothers

Blue Beginnings Publishing
Sherman Oaks, California

Published by:

Blue Beginnings Publishing
P.O. Box 304
Van Nuys, California 91405

Cover art by Rachel Hobreigh.
Cover design and typography by California Imaging.
Photograph on back cover by Jerry Harper.

Special thanks to my husband, Kevin, for his patience and encouragement. Acknowledgment is also made to James and Cheryl Nixon, Meg Florio, Jan Young, Jean Akers, Arlene Wheeler, Carolyn Holmes and Leslie Coloco for their generous help.

ISBN: 0-9639528-0-3
Library of Congress Card Number: 93-074144

First Printing.
Printed in the United States of America.

In memory of my father and mother, Frank Holmes and Jean Valentine, who told me to aspire.

WHITE TRASH

Chapter One

Gretchen Carey poured herself another cup of coffee and pushed open the slate-blue, chintz curtains of the east bay window in her kitchen. Ominous thunderclouds mounted on the horizon, but a stream of sunlight broke through and struck the little papier-maché zebra on the sill. She had finished painting the black stripes last night, and the glazed surface gleamed like enamel. Later, she would place it in Julia's room, on the scalloped, short white shelf over the window. A lion and an elephant, earlier projects from last year, already adorned the shelf like a tiny, exotic menagerie.

"Mommy?" Julia approached, a solemn ragamuffin in her brown plaid robe, her eyes almost obscured by her halo of red hair. "Can we go to the park?"

"If it doesn't rain first, sugar," Gretchen said. Her speech still carried the easy inflections from her childhood in Oklahoma. Sometimes she thought she almost fit into Los Angeles, until she spoke and someone commented on her accent. Then the loneliness would return, and the longing for home.

"Where's Bucky?" Gretchen asked.

"He's playing with his blocks in his room. When can we go to the park?"

Gretchen glanced at the clock on the wall. It was almost nine-thirty. "Your daddy's supposed to call soon, when he gets out from his meeting. After that, maybe we can go." She brightened, set down her coffee and hoisted the little girl onto her hip.

"I think Daddy's got some good news from work," she said, tweaking Julia's nose.

"Are you lucky, Mommy?" The little girl regarded her mother with soft green eyes.

"Yes, sugar. Very lucky. Now go play with Bucky for a few minutes, will you?"

Carrying her mug, she passed the oak bill holder on the wall above the counter. She set down her cup and fished out the letter she had received three days ago, turning the pale pink envelope gingerly in her hands. She still had not found the courage to open it.

Why would her mother, or someone claiming to be her mother, be writing to her after all these years? Her mother had walked out when she had been twelve years old, and Ted had been eight. She would never understand, no matter what her father had said about her mother being unhappy, or having problems, or that she had just disappeared. In her mind, her mother had simply died. Living with that belief, she had found a tenuous peace.

She held the letter, staring at the tense handwriting, and imagined the envelope blowing up if she opened it. Her life would explode along with it. Fragments of pain from her childhood would rain down on her, splinters and embers from the long-ago loss. Her present life, so settled, so secure and safe, would be incinerated.

She slipped the letter back into the bill holder, out of sight, relieved to put it aside again. Not yet, she thought. I'm not ready yet. She wanted to see her children.

She found them in Bucky's room, intent on some kind of marble game with tubes and a blast-off platform. He and Julia must have been bouncing in Bucky's crib earlier, for the blue bumpers, dotted with tiny rocking horses, hung to the floor. The lambskin had been wadded into a ball in the corner, and Bolo Bear hung by one foot from the railing. Sam, undoubtedly, would say it resembled the crib of an insane, homeless baby. She stepped over to straighten the mess.

Julia patiently doled out marbles to her brother. The kids played on, oblivious of Gretchen in the room. She could have watched them for hours.

Damn right she was lucky. But she had not been stupid, either. She had always known she would find her happiness with a man, and had no shame in that. She had been lucky to meet Sam, and smart to marry him. He possessed an air of success, even before his career began to skyrocket five years ago with Titan Technologies. If he had one quality that had first hooked her, it was his confidence. The very quality, bordering on arrogance, that she had resented in the young Air Force officers who had approached her years ago in Oklahoma. She herself had been painfully lacking in such easy self-assurance, and privilege, and the promise of a brilliant future.

When she met Sam, in a different time and a different place, she had sensed this man could give her a life. She had been right. Sam loved her. She had two wonderful children and a house in one of the most desirable neighborhoods in the San Fernando Valley. If she missed Oklahoma, and her father and brother at times, it was a small price to pay for what she had. The perfect husband. The perfect life. She had played her cards right.

The shrill ringing of the phone interrupted her thoughts. She dashed into the kitchen to answer it.

"Hello?"

"Honey, are you sitting down?"

She froze. "Why...why do you ask that, Sam?"

"Gretchen...Norman didn't give me a raise."

"It's okay," she said bravely, her fingers twisting the curls at the nape of her neck. "Times are tough right now. Lots of companies are cutting back."

"Gretchen, I've been laid off."

"What?" she said faintly. His words had knocked the breath out of her chest. She was surprised she could even speak.

"Norman said the Cold War is over. It's 1990 and he has to adapt to the times. There's no future in nuclear weapons. He's converting to garbage recycling and hiring waste management engineers. I've got two weeks"

Panic enveloped her; she spun in a whirlpool of dizziness. She leaned against the counter, hot, her hands sweaty. The cream-and-blue pattern on the walls, that she had so enthusiastically sponge-painted six months ago, suddenly struck her as too busy, too complicated. She shut her eyes.

Her coffee mug slid to the tiled floor, shattering. "I've got to go," she said quickly and hung up the phone. Hot coffee scorched her ankles. Muddy-brown splotches stained the hem of her robe. A shard of pottery had nicked her shin, and a trickle of blood began to run down her leg. She stared at the mess in horror. Her children appeared at the door and watched her in silence.

Gretchen blinked, uncertain, and at that moment felt exactly as she had in Oklahoma, one night during a tornado alert. She had huddled in the shelter with her father and brother, scared for her life, the wind roaring over their heads like a freight train in the sky.

Chapter Two

How could this possibly happen to us?" Gretchen asked that evening, toying with her salad. Sam had come home late, and the children had demanded his constant attention. Finally, with the kids' dinners half-finished and their behavior turning disruptive, she had started a cartoon video for them in the den.

"Times change," Sam shrugged, as if unconcerned.

"But what will we do?"

"I don't know yet. I'll have to give it some thought."

Gretchen put down her fork. His calmness, a quality she usually found reassuring, made her want to get up and shake him. To scream at him, to shock him into alarm. From the time he had broken the news to her, she had done nothing but think about it. Her mind had been like a slide show of fearful possibilities that revolved over and over again. Click. Unemployment. Click. Unpaid bills. Click. Homelessness.

"Did you see this coming?" Gretchen pressed. "Did you expect to get fired?"

"I didn't get *fired*, Gretchen," Sam answered defensively. "I've been laid off. There's a big difference."

"Oh. You mean it's more honorable this way?"

"Well, yeah. Of course it is. Honey. Norman is getting into garbage, which has a hell of a better future these days than bombs."

She nodded, wondering if she could feel more shame, more desolation, if he had been fired. She doubted it. They had been cast out.

Her gaze strayed to the flame of the single candle that flickered between them on the oak table. "After two weeks we won't have your salary anymore." The flame blurred, and she felt herself sinking into its hypnotic dance.

"I know," he agreed. "But it's going to be fine."

He had said that two months ago when he forgot to pay the gas bill, and the company threatened to cut them off. He had made no apology, and joked about her getting hysterical when she insisted he take the payment to the office that day.

"Oh, Gretchen..." He rested his elbow on the table, cupping his chin in his hand. "It's not as if I did a terrible job. Didn't I tell you, with everything that's been happening in Europe, that this country was due for a change? When the Berlin wall fell in November...it was so remarkable."

"But not for us!" she blurted, her cheeks wet.

He reached across the table for her hand. "I know. Look, the truth is that we don't need any more bombs. There are over one hundred thousand warheads in the world. The Cold War is over."

"But you're a Republican," she said, absurdly.

"Okay, when Reagan dumped money into defense, I jumped on the bandwagon. Right or wrong. Now it's over, and we've got to change. Believe me, everyone in defense is getting hit hard right now."

"Change to what?" she asked quietly. He stroked her fingers.

He sighed, a tired breath. "I don't know. New technologies. The space program, or the environment. There are lots of possibilities. Don't worry."

His fingers traced her palm. She warmed to his touch, calmer, slightly reassured. After their five years together, and even in the current crisis of his impending layoff, she still found herself captivated by him: the feathery-blond hair, glowing in the candlelight like mother-of-pearl, the picket-white teeth, the bold blue eyes.

"Wanna party?" He smiled mischievously, as if sensing her reaction. He pulled her hand closer. She marveled at his constant ability to switch moods, to push anything at all aside to go to bed with her.

"Oh, please."

"The kids are watching T.V. Come on. I'll take your mind off your troubles."

"Jesus. Like that always solves everything." She resisted, but felt the pull of his stare. As he stroked her palm, and the inside of her fingers, a rosy heat started over her cheeks, down her throat, and her hips swiveled unconsciously toward him in her chair. She snatched her hand back as Julia entered the room.

Julia's gaze rested on Gretchen's face, then Sam's. "What are you guys talking about?" Her squeaky, four-year-old voice seemed incongruous with the mature question she asked.

Sam picked up his wine glass and said, "We're talking about Daddy's work, goofy. Where's Bucky?"

"He's washing his hands in the bathroom."

"Great," Sam said, starting to rise from his chair. "The bathroom's probably flooded by now."

"It's all right, Sam," Gretchen said quickly. Suddenly her tension felt unbearable, and she longed for yesterday, when life had been easy and predictable. "Julia, bring him out of there, will you, sugar?" She tried to keep her voice patient, but Julia glanced at her in surprise. She forced a smile. "And turn off the water."

"Okay," Julia said compliantly. She padded toward the hall, chubby in her light-blue cotton leggings and tent blouse. Moments later she returned, clutching her protesting two-year-old brother against her chest. "Not fair. Not fair!"

Where Bucky was a miniature of his father, with wispy blond hair and crystal-blue eyes that could melt the reserve of the most unapproachable creature on earth, Julia favored Gretchen. Gretchen was thoroughly pleased that Julia had inherited her own wide-spaced green eyes, heart-shaped face and curly auburn hair, which both of them wore to the collar. She was grateful that Julia, like herself, would be spared the lifelong ordeal of curling irons, perms and hair spray that most women seemed to endure.

Sam snapped his fingers. "I forgot. I bought something for you two." He rose from his chair and reached for a plastic bag on the coffee table. "The Wizard of Oz," he said, holding up the movie. "This was a favorite of mine when I was a little boy. Do you want to watch it?"

"Is it scary?" Julia asked, typically suspicious.

"There's a scary witch or two. Mommy or I can sit with you if you get scared. Come on, I'll put it on for you. I guess I'll watch the movie with them for a while," he said to his wife. "Want to come?"

"In a bit," Gretchen replied. She finished her dinner and washed the dishes. Then she sank into the brown leather couch in the living room, relieved to have a few moments to herself after a full day with the kids. She stared out the new, white French doors to the back patio beyond, shrouded in dense darkness. She thought about bombs and small children, the glad, singing voices of the munchkins filling her ears from the room beyond.

As she put Julia to bed later, the little girl asked, "Mommy, can I watch that movie tomorrow?"

"The Wizard of Oz? Sure, sugar. You can watch it after you come home from school. I saw that movie when I was a little girl."

"Your daddy bought it for you?"

Gretchen laughed. "No, silly. We didn't have VCRs. I saw it on television, usually around Christmas. But I remember Dorothy, and the Tin Man, and especially the Cowardly Lion."

"Mommy?" Julia lay still on her side, small in the full-sized canopy bed Sam had bought for her several months ago. Gretchen pulled the white coverlet closer around the little girl's chin. Pink and white butterflies, rimming the top of the walls, glowed in the soft beam of a clown night light. Outside, rain began to fall in a soft pattering.

"Yes, sugar."

"I love Dorothy."

Gretchen chuckled. "Do you?"

"Can I meet her?" Julia's green eyes sought her mother's, her gaze serious and imploring.

"Well...Dorothy is really a little girl named Judy Garland. People pretend to be other people in the movies. That's their work. It's kind of complicated. Do you understand, a little?"

"Can I meet the girl who plays Dorothy?"

Gretchen sighed. "No. I wish you could, but Judy Garland grew up into a big lady. Then she died."

Julia fell silent for a moment. "How did she die?" Julia's experience with death had been limited to pill bugs and a bird in the street, bloody and smashed flat by passing cars.

"Um. She was unhappy. She took too much medicine once, and she died."

"Oh."

Gretchen sensed her daughter's disappointment. Julia was a child who took things hard. "Isn't it wonderful, though, that we'll always have Dorothy in the movie?" she asked cheerfully, then kissed her on the cheek. "Good night, sugar. I love you."

Gretchen found Sam in his office, typing on his computer keyboard.

"I think Julia's sad," she told him. She plunked down in one of the yellow Queen Anne chairs across from the desk. The house had turned cool. She buttoned her blue cardigan and stretched out her legs, snug in her gray wool slacks.

"Hmm. Maybe you're right," Sam said, still typing. "Do you think she misses Lisa?"

Lisa, Julia's best friend for the last year, had recently moved from the neighborhood with her family.

"I know she does," Gretchen sighed. "I wish she didn't have to learn about friends moving away, or people dying."

"Who died?"

"Oh, I told her about Judy Garland. I couldn't explain suicide, of course. That would have made no sense to her. But she understands that Dorothy is dead, and I could tell she's sad."

"She'll forget about it," Sam said.

"I guess." Gretchen remained vaguely troubled about Julia. Her daughter was beginning to understand the realities of life, that people left and died. Soon she would learn that Sam was out of work, and that their lives might change.

"Sam?"

He didn't seem to hear.

"Sam, why do you have a wife and kids when all you want to do is relate to your computer?"

He grinned at her. She smiled back. He subscribed to a computer mailbox and wrote inane letters, every chance he got, to strangers all over the world whom he would never meet.

"I'm scared, Sam. I'm really scared."

"A toughie like you? Haven't I always taken care of you?"

She gathered her thoughts. "I don't want to be poor again. I thought that life was behind me."

Sam laughed abruptly. "My God, it's not that bad, Gretchen! I've always landed on my feet, haven't I? Have a little faith in me."

"Oh, it's not that! I'm sorry, I didn't mean..." She should have known he would take her fears personally. He often did. "You've never been laid off before, that's all."

He looked her in the eye. "Gretchen," he said firmly. "I have always taken care of this family. You've got to leave this to me. I know what I'm doing."

"Okay," she said quietly, and wondered what other choice she had. Resentment flared for an instant, then guilt. She knew he was right. He had taken care of her.

Still, as on occasional moments, she thought about how his choices had affected her life. How his prosperity had been hers as well, and that now, her and her children's futures depended on his next decisions. When she considered her marriage like that she had a sense of plummeting, of her life careening out of her control.

"Honey, I'm tired," he said, interrupting her thoughts. "I'm just going to go to bed. Are you coming?"

"In a while," she said, relieved. She didn't want to make love. She stared out the picture window. The view of the valley was panoramic; the shadows of the mountains hovered beyond, looming against a bed of sizzling lights below. She had wanted the house for this view.

Sam waited at the door. "Did you open the letter from your mother yet?" he asked gently.

"No," she said, eyes steady. Rivulets of rain began to stream down the glass. "I will soon, though."

"It's been sitting in the bill holder for three days."

"I know. I'll be along soon, Sam."

"Okay. What's that stuff in the trash bags near the front door?"

"Old clothes for the Blind People. They're going to have a truck in the neighborhood tomorrow."

The Blind Association of Los Angeles County, she simplified to the Blind People. The Trash People came on Tuesdays. The Potty People fixed the toilet the last time Bucky tried to flush a diaper. And she steadfastly made regular donations to the Elephant People, who were trying to save the African elephant from extinction; a tragedy that moved her to tears.

"I hope you didn't give them my best pants this time."

"No, it's old stuff of the kids, Sam. I promise."

He went to bed and she breathed deeply, completely alone for the first time all day. The rain fell gently outside. She closed her eyes, thinking of Oklahoma.

She had been ten when her family returned from Okinawa. Her father, a master sergeant in the Air Force, had orders for a four-year assignment at Tinker Air Force Base near Oklahoma City.

She couldn't remember much before her mother left. She had a vague recollection of the base housing, and the identical low stucco houses. The barking dogs on chains. The red clay, like silt, that her mother struggled to remove from their clothes during the spring dust storms. Two big fans had been their only defense against the oppressive heat and humidity in the summer. Her father's old white sedan, dented on the top from a hail storm, slithered and slid on the icy roads in the winter. Her mother dragged her like a limp doll through a thick wall of wind.

Gretchen went into the kitchen and picked up the letter. Seventeen years. Her mother was from another lifetime, and had nothing to do with her life today. She carried the letter back to Sam's office. She opened the file cabinet and pulled out a small, black-and-white photo.

Her mother smiled broadly at the camera, her teeth big and white. Her curly hair had been pulled into a ponytail. She held Gretchen, seven and dressed in a yellow satin dress, on her lap. Her father, Howard, in uniform, beamed at the camera with Ted on his knee. Ted was caught leaning over, looking down to the side, as if he had dropped something next to his father's shoe.

Gretchen peered at her mother's face. She seemed tired, her cheeks thin, but still genuinely happy and proud of her family.

She was only twenty-six in the picture, Gretchen thought, younger than I am now. What had happened to her? She tried to imagine Carole with her and Ted as children. She remembered her mother being kind, but sick a lot. She spent long hours in bed, with an odor like vomit, asking to be left alone. Her father's distance pervaded the house like a silent accusation. She and Ted trod carefully, sensing the unhappiness, the disappointment.

Her father said her mother had been unhappy for years. He explained that she drank. Harold reassured Gretchen and Ted that it wasn't their fault Carole left. Gretchen didn't understand the reasons. Only that she felt a part of a giant failure.

For the first few years, time took on a numbing, surreal quality. She might have been waiting for her, or simply in shock. She couldn't remember. She lived, unnoticed by her overwhelmed father, with the pervasive guilt and shame. She was a victim, she was a colluder. Somehow, she was responsible. Why else had she been abandoned?

Later, Gretchen had been too busy taking care of Ted and her dad to think much about her mother. After school she would leave Ted with the next door neighbors, then pedal on her bike to the commissary or base exchange to pick up whatever they needed.

That was the best part of her day. She could forget all else but the smooth motion beneath her as she steered by the shabby houses surrounded by oak and elm trees. The clothes lines hung with T-shirts and socks seemed so white against the steely sky, the only divider of the lawns that merged in a long, rectangular swath behind the houses. The air smelled of jet exhaust and greasy hamburgers from the base chow hall. Planes often rumbled in the background. Smells and sounds that became comforting and familiar as the years passed.

She put down the photo and ripped open the letter. She read quickly, hands shaking, her breath tight in her chest.

Dear Gretchen, *Jan 7, 1990*

I have no right to ask, but I want to see you. When I spoke to your father, after all these years, he said you were married, with two children. I know you could never forgive me for leaving you so long ago. I don't expect that. Maybe someday I can try to explain. If you want to get in touch with me, you can write to the address I've provided, or even call me.

Hoping to hear from you,
Mother

Gretchen folded the letter carefully and placed it on Sam's desk. She walked softly to the children's rooms, and watched each sleeping child for several minutes.

Sam lay on his side at the edge of the bed, his breathing deep and regular. She pushed the window halfway open, and cool air drifted into the room. The rain fell loudly, and the air smelled acrid with eucalyptus.

She dressed for bed, then slipped under the covers and lay stiffly on her back. Her stomach churned, heavy and stagnant. After what seemed like forever, she fell into a light sleep. Images of her life, from today and long ago, spattered across the landscape of her dreams. Elusive pictures drifted through her mind, unfocused and unclear.

Sometime in the night, the muted shades of her dream turned to rose. As a child during an Oklahoma spring, warmed and content, she lay with her head on her mother's lap and gazed up at the blooming flowers of the redbud tree. A tree that turned bare through the winter, then burst into red and pink blossoms. Only later came the appearance of the shiny green leaves, leaves that were shaped like imperfect hearts.

Chapter Three

Saturday morning, Sam and Gretchen took the children to Hancock Park to see the La Brea Tar Pits. The air smelled fresh and cool after the last night's rain, and the sky was a gray smear, torn by patches of blue. The kids wandered ahead along the fence that separated the park from the lakes of tar. A thin layer of water covered the tar. The children pointed at the statues of mammoths and shrieked at the bubbles that oozed up from the black goo.

"I've made up my mind. I'm going to start my own business," Sam announced suddenly.

"You're going to do *what*?" Gretchen stopped walking, whipped off her sun glasses and gaped at him.

Sam seemed equally stunned by her reaction. He stepped back to face her. "What does that mean?" he asked angrily. "Why the hell shouldn't I start my own business?"

Intimidated, she said, "Sam, it's just that so many businesses fail. We've gotten used to such security. The idea of starting your own business is such a...surprise, that's all."

Sam pushed back the strands of blond hair that had fallen over his forehead. "Okay. But you don't have to sound like it's the last thing in the world I can do."

Gretchen bit her lip. Sam's pride must be suffering after being laid off, whether he admitted it or not. She would have to be more supportive. Still, the idea of a business scared her. She had naturally assumed, after their discussion two days ago, that he would look for another job. Although he had occasionally mentioned starting his own business over the years, she had never taken the idea seriously.

The kids hooked their fingers through the fence and pressed their faces against the coils. Gretchen and Sam strolled up next to the children. Gretchen shoved her hands into the pockets of her overcoat. Her breath turned misty in the cold, January air.

"Well, what kind of business are you going to start, then?" she asked, realizing she had absolutely no idea what he would do. An absurd image of homemade bombs came instantly to mind, and she shuddered.

"I want to market a fuzzy logic application," Sam said. He pulled against the fence, bracing his weight.

"Fuzzy logic?" Gretchen said, her anxiety rising.

"I've been using the computer for years, as a hobbyist. I know how to program. Fuzzy logic is an up-and-coming concept."

"Yes but, what's fuzzy logic?"

"Fuzzy logic is the science of nondeterministic logic. You have high and low acceptance curves. A computer program processes a set of inputs, then weighs those inputs according to where the data lies on the two curves."

Gretchen twisted a curl of hair around her finger. "What exactly are you going to sell?"

"There are lots of possible applications. I'm interested in developing a program that would control the force used by automobile brakes. In other words, a way to make car brakes more efficient."

"Wouldn't you have to know something about cars, though?" Sam knew almost nothing about cars.

He waved his hand in an airy gesture. "Naw. I can get a mechanic to help me with the specifics. I think this idea could really take off, honey."

Pushing her fears aside for the present, Gretchen reached for his hand. "If anyone can make a business succeed, you can, Sam."

He squeezed her hand. "I'll get started on a plan tomorrow, then we'll apply for a small business loan. I know it's hard to believe now, but I think this layoff could be the best thing that's ever happened to us. The start of a whole new career for me. My own business."

She leaned against him, encouraged by his excitement, yet wishing she felt as confident.

"Bucky! Julia! Don't throw rocks in there," Sam yelled. "Darn those kids."

"They're only little children, Sam," Gretchen said mildly.

"They could behave better. Sometimes I feel like a fish."

"A fish?"

He turned his head toward her, straight-faced. "You know. I've spawned. Now I'm deteriorating, fast. Like a salmon."

"Oh." Gretchen frowned. She attributed Sam's irritation with the children to his being an only child. He had been delighted when she had been pregnant with Julia, then less enthusiastic during her second pregnancy. He could be a wonderful father, but quick to reprimand, which troubled her at times.

"Let's go over to the museum," Sam said. "I think the kids will like seeing all those mammoth bones."

As Sam and Gretchen walked down the path and the children trailed behind, Gretchen said, "I opened the letter."

She studied Sam's face, and could tell that what she had said had not registered. If only she had a close woman friend, she thought whimsically. A friend who cared enough to remember something as important as a letter from a mother she hadn't seen in seventeen years. But she had decided long ago not to hold Sam's absent mindedness, his seeming lack of concern, against him.

"The letter from my mother, Sam," she reminded him.

"Of course," Sam said too quickly, and she forgave him again.

"What did she say?"

"She wants to see me," Gretchen said softly. She thought of the letter, and again felt the cautious excitement, and the fear.

Still walking, Sam put his arm around her and pulled her close. She could tell he didn't know what to say.

"I haven't decided what to do."

"Well, I think it's great!" Sam said, his tone effervescent. "She's your mother. You're going to get in touch with her, aren't you?"

"Not necessarily!" she retorted, irritated by his assumptions. "Why should I?"

The children waited for them at the base of the ramp leading up to the museum, hand in hand. Except in size, they were identical in their blue parkas, with the hoods pulled snugly over their heads. Gretchen stopped walking.

"Because she's your mother," he said. "If she were my mother, I'd want to see her."

Something about his expression–in a face glowing with privilege–exasperation, smugness, criticism, suddenly made her feel worlds away from him.

"You don't know what you're talking about," she said icily. "How could you possibly know?" She turned away from him and walked briskly toward her children.

"I know you're scared, Gretchen," she heard him call after her. "You always get angry like this when you're scared."

❆ ❆ ❆

"What are all these bones?" Julia asked in a small voice. They had stopped in front of a long glass case containing hundreds of identical, ancient wolf skulls. She stood between Sam and Gretchen, her hood flung off and her parka unzipped.

"What're bones, Mommy?" Bucky, on Sam's shoulders, mimicked his sister.

The children had seemed only mildly interested in the statues of reconstructed mammoth bones in the center of the museum, the sloths and prehistoric birds.

"These are all the bones of the animals who fell into the tar pits," Gretchen answered. She had assumed Julia understood when she explained earlier. Yet, she reconsidered. Of course the concepts of distant time, and death on such a mass scale, must be mysterious to Julia.

"The real big bones that we saw, those were dinosaurs," Gretchen added, hoping Julia could relate from the images she had seen in cartoons and picture books.

"Mammoths," Sam corrected her. "It's a common misconception that dinosaurs fell into the tar pits."

Julia continued to stare at the skulls, frowning.

"Millions of years ago, the tar was covered with water, like it is today," Sam added. "The animals went to get a drink, then got stuck in the tar."

"But, what happened to the animals?" Julia asked in her squeaky, serious voice.

"Well, they died, sweetie," Sam answered. "All that's left is their bones. People dug the bones out of the tar and put them in the museum."

"In the mutheum," Bucky echoed.

"But what happened to their skin?" Julia asked.

Gretchen glanced at Sam.

"When animals die, their skin falls off. All that's left is the bones," Sam said, shifting his weight back and forth, Bucky's arms encircling his head.

"Their skin falls off!" Julia's voice rose in horror.

"Thkin falthoff!" Bucky cried.

"Shut up, stupid! You don't even know what we're talking about." Julia glared up at Bucky.

"Kids. Come on!" Sam scolded.

"Julia. When an animal dies, everything goes back to the earth except the bones. The bones stay like they are for a very long time," Gretchen tried to explain.

"What if I fall in a tar pit?" Julia asked, close to tears.

"Oh, Julia," Sam said. "Nowadays, people don't fall in tar pits. We know better. And there are fences, remember?"

Why then, Gretchen thought glumly, do I feel like I have one foot in a tar pit?

She stared at the rows of snarling, defiant skulls, the sole remnants of the fierce animals that had once roamed the earth. Beautiful in their simplicity and durability, glowing and luminous inside the clear glass. These bones, the framework of life, had survived through the ages.

For a moment she considered the relentless passage of time, like a caustic tide, and her own, brief life as it played out before her. She wondered what she had learned, and what she could teach her children about the rhythms and complexities of life. Mysteries of which she had so little understanding. Why does everything change? Why do people die? Why do they leave?

"Does it hurt when the skin falls off?" Julia asked, and Gretchen's attention riveted back to her daughter.

"Oh, no!" Gretchen assured her. "And isn't it wonderful, to still have the bones of animals that lived millions of years ago? When I see these bones I feel like I can almost–reach back and touch the living wolves, and the tigers and birds. Can't you just imagine what they were like?" Noting Julia's suspicious, dour expression, Gretchen added quickly, "And the animals are in heaven, of course. It's only their bodies that go back to the earth."

"For God's sakes," Sam said.

"Just because you're an atheist, you don't have to make them grow up like you," Gretchen shot back.

Sam shook his head. "Saber-toothed tigers in heaven? I think you lived in the Bible Belt for a little too long, baby."

Chapter Four

That night, after putting the kids to bed, Sam and Gretchen relaxed in the office. As usual, Sam turned on his computer. Gretchen leafed through a travel magazine.

"I'm starting my business plan," Sam explained.

"That's okay," Gretchen said. He knew she resented the computer–he turned it on every chance he got–and was often apologetic. She had no interest or inclination to learn how to use his computer, as much as he encouraged her.

"You can communicate with people all over the world on any subject," Sam would say. "There's a wealth of information that you can access from your own home."

"Who would I write letters to, and what about?" she had asked once, humoring him.

"Your hobbies!"

"My hobbies. What are my hobbies?"

"Well," he had appeared to be searching. "You know. Papier-maché. And...and...guns!"

She burst out laughing. "Papier-maché, maybe. Not my guns. My dad taught me how to shoot. Lots of people know how to shoot."

"I never knew a woman who had guns, though," he said, a touch of grudging admiration in his voice.

Her father had given her a .38 special with a gold trigger and ivory handles, and she would never give it up. She wanted to replace the ivory with wood, but her father wouldn't hear of it.

She also had a 30-06 lever-action saddle rifle that had belonged to her grandfather. She kept both guns locked in a cabinet, out of reach in the spare bedroom.

Sam didn't approve of her guns, initially citing the dangers of a loaded gun in the house. She had been adamant. Her father had always kept guns, and had taught her about safety. And living in Los Angeles, with the long hours that Sam often worked, she simply felt safer. Occasionally, she would shoot the .38 at a firing range, just to stay in practice.

"I don't like computers," she had said. "I can't understand the pleasure of writing letters to people I'll never meet. If I have any spare time, I'd rather spend it with my family."

He had instantly risen to sit with her. She knew he hated it when she was mad at him.

Now, as he continued to work on his business plan, she determined to not make him feel guilty. She reached behind her and took one of her papier-maché animals from a shelf. She made miniature elephants, rhinos, zebras and leopards. She sculpted African animals whose persecution and suffering haunted her day and night.

She had learned to make papier-maché objects in a craft class. Julia had been delighted by her first animal, a little dog. She had naturally continued to make the animals she loved, and had a cherished collection scattered along the shelves of the house.

She set the elephant carefully back on the shelf. Sam typed quickly, his eyes fixed on his computer screen. Restless, she picked up a legal pad from his desk and began composing a letter to her mother.

"I hate you. You must be the worst mother in the world," she began, then tried again.

"It's great to hear from you, Mother. Of course, we should get together soon." Then, "Please do not try and contact me again. What you did is unforgivable, whatever your reasons. No real mother could ever abandon her own children."

Tears filled her eyes, and her next lines ended in scribbles. A soft moan came to her lips, and she dropped the pen and covered her face with her hands.

"Honey! What is it?" Sam sprang up from behind the desk, slipping into the chair next to hers.

Savagely Gretchen yanked a tissue from the box on the desk. "I feel stupid. I shouldn't let this upset me."

"Of course you're upset. It's about your mother, isn't it? I'm sure it must be–shocking to hear from her like this."

"I thought she was dead!" Gretchen said in hoarse sobs, gesturing with open palms. "At least, that's what I came to believe. Why else would she have...disappeared for so many years? I never had any hope of ever seeing her again."

"But aren't you glad?" he asked, his voice careful. "That your mother is alive, and wants to see you?"

"Yeah. I guess," she said, more calmly. She turned to her husband, wanting him to understand. "My mother's a stranger to me, Sam. I barely remember her. She abandoned me when I was a child. Try and think what that means. How would Julia and Bucky feel if I left, and never came back? How do you think I felt, as a little girl?"

"Pretty terrible, I'll bet," he said soberly. "You've never talked about it much."

He took her hand and laced her fingers with his own.

"I think I'll call her. I will," she said, in control again. "Don't you think I should?"

"It's up to you, babe," he said, his voice gentle.

"Maybe she's a really nice lady. Maybe there's something I don't know, about why she left."

"But I thought your dad said..."

She stared at him, green eyes moist and glittering. "My dad said she was unhappy. Then after a while, he just avoided my questions. Almost like there was something he didn't want me to know."

"Well, maybe it would be good if you talked to her. At least you could find out what happened."

"Yeah, Sam. I'll call her. I will. Maybe not tomorrow, but I will." She smiled up at him, and he pulled her into his lap.

They listened to the clear tones of the classical CD Sam had put on earlier. Sam loved classical music, and was a fair pianist. He had inherited his piano from his beloved Grandfather Buchanan. It took up most of the living room, black and hulking, with its chipped ivory keys that Sam refused to replace with plastic.

"This room sure is a mess," Gretchen said suddenly, taking in the shoes on the floor, the toys on the desk and the empty glasses.

They both laughed.

"Why don't you get a housekeeper?" Sam asked, as he had many times before. "It's hard taking care of the kids, and a big house like this."

Sam was being kind, she knew. She simply was not a good housekeeper, and of course had never had a mother to help her learn. Howard and Ted never minded clutter and a mess, but Sam certainly did. She had done better in their apartment, but then she had only Julia to care for. Their new house, which they had moved into shortly before Bucky was born, consisted of five bedrooms, a study, a den, a living room and formal dining room. A sprawling, grassy backyard extended from the patio, and always needed weeding. Gretchen hated to have a stranger in her house, going through her things. But recently her neighbor, Paula, had urged her to get some help.

"You'll never believe this, but I called an agency last week," she told Sam. "Paula gave me the number. A woman is supposed to come over Thursday for me to meet."

"That's great," Sam said enthusiastically.

"Oh. I wonder if I should cancel, though," she said, suddenly worried.

"Why?"

"Well...I don't know how the money's going to work out for a while."

"Absolutely not," Sam said magnanimously. "We have plenty in savings, and I estimate this business will be rolling in about three months."

"That quickly?" she asked, surprised.

"Sure! I've been thinking about it for days. I'll have to develop the program, then we'll rent an office and buy some computer equipment. This product is simple, but powerful."

Gretchen knew nothing about business, but trusted that Sam did. Their savings account held ten thousand dollars. It wasn't enough to make her feel secure, but still, there was no immediate crisis.

Unwilling to undermine her husband, she said, "Okay. Then I'll go ahead and have the housekeeper come."

"Great! Some help around the house will make things a lot easier for you, honey. I know it."

They listened to the music, and Gretchen felt content for the first time in days. She would call her mother soon, and give her a chance to explain. Suddenly, she felt hopeful. Maybe she could have a new relationship with her mother, a new start.

As if sensing her optimistic mood, Sam hugged her tightly. "My generic wife," he said playfully. "How old are you now?"

"Twenty-nine," she reminded him. "Why do you call me that? Like I could be...anyone."

"It's a compliment!" He kissed her back, between her shoulder blades. "You're the embodiment of all women. Sensuous, beautiful, nurturing and smart." He wrapped his arms around her waist. "That's why I married you. All women should be like you. Twenty-nine?" He sounded surprised. "*Nobody's* twenty-nine. You still look great, honey."

She leaned against him, pleased. "I go to the gym every chance I get, and I stay out of the sun."

Gretchen knew he appreciated her, even if she didn't have the education he had. He rarely patronized her. He had wanted someone clear-headed, steady and intelligent. She had possessed those qualities. During their five years of marriage she had been consistent and loving. She maintained a calming presence to his passions and mood swings, his humor and excitements, and his occasionally volatile temper.

After a few moments Sam lay his cheek against her back and asked softly, "How do you feel?"

Gretchen lowered her lashes, knowing he wanted sex. She liked sex with Sam, but felt so tired much of the time. Between the house and the kids, the laundry and the shopping, by the end of the day she was usually worn out. Sometimes she joked with Sam, to his dismay, that when she was tired her sex drive was the first thing to go and the last to come back.

To her astonishment, a few months after Bucky was born when she had been especially tired, Sam presented her with several poster boards showing charts and graphs of her menstrual cycle. Pointing at the intersecting lines representing her hormones, he had said in desperation, "But you're *supposed* to be interested now!"

Now, as the music filled her ears and he waited for an answer, she longed for his arms around her and his body next to hers. Her entire world had been shaken, in less than a week, with Sam's layoff and the letter from her mother. She felt split apart, the security and comfort of her life changed irrevocably. But she still had her kids, and her husband. She needed his comfort.

"I feel pretty good, Sam," she said spiritedly. "Let's go to bed."

❄ ❄ ❄

In the early morning hours, Gretchen woke abruptly. She listened in the darkness, and heard Julia crying. Bolting out of bed, she ran into the child's room.

"It's okay. Mommy's here," Gretchen soothed, gathering the little girl into her arms. "My goodness. What's the matter?"

"Mommy," Julia sobbed. "I don't want my skin to fall off. I don't want to die."

"Oh, sugar," Gretchen said, smoothing her hair. "You're not going to die for a very, very long time. You're just a little girl. You don't need to worry about things like that."

Julia hiccupped, then her breathing slowed and became regular. Gretchen continued to hold her, rocking gently. She wished she had more power over events that were out of her control. If only she were better at being a mother. At being a wife. She stared between the curtains of Julia's window, into the black, moonless night. A mockingbird screamed, its voice like shrill bullets. Then it cooed, imploring peals. Jungle sounds.

Lacking in tools she should have learned from her mother, Gretchen relied on her love, eternal and pulsing. Love that kept her sadness at bay, and made her life worth living. Love that no one could ever take away.

Chapter Five

What a big sweaty mess," Sam remarked a few days later as he stood on his front porch and surveyed his neighborhood. It was eight o'clock in the morning. He had dressed in a tan suit that complemented his blond hair, and a gold-and-red striped tie. He held a steaming mug of coffee in one hand. Even though he had only one week left at his job, he appeared as professional as ever.

He watched as a pair of scruffy motorcyclists, with bandannas around their heads, roared past and pulled into the Rialto's house on the corner. Danny Rialto and his wife had moved several months ago, and the house had stood vacant. Now, a pickup truck had been making trips since yesterday, unloading furniture.

"What do you mean, Sam?" Gretchen asked. She sat in the white porch swing, bundled against the January cold in her robe, drinking coffee. Bucky wasn't up yet. Julia was inside, eating cereal.

"This neighborhood! My God, if this is one of the better ones in the valley, then we're in trouble," he said with disdain.

"Think about our illustrious neighbors. Mrs. Doheny, across the street, electrocuted her husband years ago by turning on the pool light while he indulged in a midnight swim. Some kind of short, I understand. Now she wears rubber gloves everywhere she goes. Then there's the Bender family. You know, the psychopath with the shotgun rack on the back of his truck, who screams at his girls night and day and has a face like a pit bull. And Mary Ellen, who's got to be thirty-five, and lives with her mother. Didn't you tell me she washes her hands fifty times a day? All she does is scew the Lasser boy, whenever his parents aren't home. That couple on the corner gets the grand prize. I've been tempted to snatch a copy of the Anarchy Express from the stacks on their porch when I jog by. You call this street typical?"

"Well, I don't know..."

"I haven't even mentioned Paula, your manic friend next door. She's missing some marbles, I'd say. And I have a pretty good idea what our new neighbors at the Rialto house will be like. Motorcyclists from hell."

"Sam, really," Gretchen said. Before Bucky was born they had lived in an apartment on the West Side, surrounded mostly by professional people. With two children, they had needed a house. Sam had taken suburbia hard. Although the area was expensive, most of the neighbors had bought thirty years ago and retired, or else had given their homes to their children.

Sam had actually tried to be friendly, but had gotten into continual disputes with the neighbors over barking dogs off leashes, loud music and speeding cars without mufflers. To Gretchen's disappointment, he had come to dismiss the neighbors as illiterate imbeciles.

Gretchen kept to herself, but liked to maintain friendly relations with the neighbors. They didn't seem all that different from her neighbors in Oklahoma, when she had lived in base housing. If she had one misgiving, it was that there were not more children on the block. Paula, her next door neighbor, had a son. But Paula worked, and Joey went to day care every day.

Sam continued to rave. "Sweetheart, we could compete with Storybook Lane this year. Some night next December I'm going to sneak out and hang huge signs on each end of the block that say, 'DYSFUNCTIONAL FAMILY LANE'. People from all over L.A. will cruise our street. They'll peer into the houses and try to get a glimpse, a picture, of the deranged lives inside. Our neighborhood will be famous, you'll see, even if not for the most conventional reasons."

"Jesus, Sam." Gretchen's eyes narrowed. "What's the matter with you?"

"I have a toothache."

Gretchen tensed. "Oh, God. Not again. You just had that root canal last month!"

Even with the dental plan that Titan Technologies provided, Gretchen sent Dr. Mosier an average of two hundred dollars a month for Sam's dental work. She had done so for over three years, ever since Sam's old fillings had started to fall out, or needed replacing due to age.

Sam had the worst teeth of anyone she had ever known. Almost every one of his teeth had been filled, root canaled, or capped. Sam admitted to overdoing sweets as an adolescent, and practicing poor dental care. Dr. Mosier attributed Sam's problems to luck of the draw, simple heredity.

Sam maintained scrupulous dental habits, even to the extent of carrying a gold-plated, rubber-tipped gum stimulator at all times in his shirt pocket with his pens. When someone asked him for a pen, he was just as likely to hand them his gum stimulator. He massaged his gums in the car, while waiting for Gretchen in bed, or when he watched television. Still, healthy teeth and gums eluded him.

"What do you think the problem is?" Gretchen asked, hopeful that it was something simple and inexpensive.

"I'm pretty sure it's the tooth with the new crown," Sam said, massaging his lower left jaw.

"How can that be? That crown was four hundred dollars! I'm still paying it off!"

Sam shrugged. "The root can still become diseased. No dentist can guarantee that won't happen. If I'm right about this tooth, Dr. Mosier will have to take off the crown and do a root canal."

After so much experience with toothaches, Sam was usually accurate about the source.

She had begun telling Julia at an early age: "You can marry a man with good teeth just as easily as you can marry a man with poor teeth," lest her daughter ever be plagued with the same, seemingly endless financial drain.

She insisted that Julia and Bucky brush their teeth after every meal and after sweets, unwilling to allow her children to befall the same dental fate as Sam. When she sat for a friend's little boy, the same age as Julia, Gretchen made him brush his teeth with a spare toothbrush, just on the remote possibility that this child should ever grow up and marry her daughter.

"I'll call Dr. Mosier," Sam said, still rubbing his jaw.

"Do what you have to do."

❄ ❄ ❄

After Sam left, Gretchen sat at the table and browsed through the paper. Bucky, beside her in his high chair, ate honey toast with the crusts trimmed off.

"Mommy, am I going to school today?" Julia asked, her curly hair messy. She wore her brown plaid robe and droopy brown socks. She perched on the leather couch, leafing through a picture book.

"No, sugar," Gretchen answered, her eyes drifting over the front page of the paper. "Today's Monday. You go to school Tuesdays and Thursdays."

"What are we going to do today?" Julia asked.

"I have to run some errands. Then I thought we might go to the park. Would you like that?"

"Uh-huh. Mommy, can I watch the Wizard of Oz?"

Gretchen hesitated. She didn't like the kids watching so much television, although Sam didn't seem to mind. Still, the movie was a wonderful classic, and she wouldn't be ready to go out for an hour or so.

"Sure. I'll put it on for you."

"Is Dorothy dead, Mommy?" Julia asked as Gretchen rewound the tape in the den.

"Judy Garland is dead, sugar," Gretchen answered patiently. "Dorothy will always be in the movie."

"Did her skin fall off?" Julia asked.

"I guess," Gretchen said, wondering if death was becoming a preoccupation.

"Here you go, kid." Gretchen pressed the play button and left the room. Bucky was putting bits of toast into his juice cup.

"Okay, buddy. I think you're done."

Bucky slid from the high chair, still in his footed pajamas. He sank to the rug and began pulling some large colored beads apart. Where Julia liked being near Gretchen, and seemed to have an introspective, cautious view of the world, Bucky was more self-sufficient and leaped into activities and play.

Left alone, Gretchen browsed through the remainder of the paper. Those Nursery School People, the McMartin family, had filed suit. The Soviet army met with strong resistance in Armenia and Azerbayan. Protestors had been arrested at the Federal building, marching against the United States' policy in El Salvador. The California legislature voted to restore twenty million for family planning. An article about the terrible Iranian earthquake occupied the left column. Economic indicators predicted a recession, and the housing market had turned sluggish.

The drought continued, with talk of water rationing. Turning the pages, she stopped cold at a full-page picture of a dead elephant, its face hacked off. Shocked, tears came to her eyes, and she stared at the picture in horrible fascination.

There is so much grief and misery on the planet, she thought, and especially for animals. She turned the page, unable to bear the picture a moment longer. She would be sure to send the Elephant People more money, she resolved. Even with the new status of elephants as an endangered species, illegal poaching continued. What would finally bring the killing to an end?

After a few moments she glanced at other articles, all disjointed, all to be continued on another page. She wondered where her own life fit in, like an article in the swirling black-and-white print. Gretchen Carey, housewife, life disrupted. Husband laid off. Future unknown. Her happiness and security to be continued, if and when Sam made a real start of his business.

Brooding with the uncertainties of her life, she rose and found the letter from her mother in Sam's office. She hesitated, putting it down, then picked it up again. Steeling herself, she grabbed the phone and dialed the number in Texas her mother had provided. Her stomach clenched, and her hands felt moist.

"Hello?" a woman answered.

Gretchen's breath stopped. "I'm looking for Carole Simpson."

"Yes!"

"Are you Carole Simpson?" Gretchen asked weakly.

A brief silence. "I am. Oh my God...is this...?"

Gretchen took a step back. "This is Gretchen Carey," she said stiffly, unprepared for the intensity of emotion on the other line. And the voice, with a disturbing hint of familiarity. "I got your letter..."

Gretchen could hear soft weeping.

"Thank you for calling. I didn't know if..."

"You didn't know?"

"If you hated me," the woman said, her voice breaking.

"Look, I don't remember you very well, okay?"

"Of course you don't." The woman's voice rang of loss, of hopelessness, of unbearable grief.

"Why did you write me now?" Gretchen blurted out. "Where have you been?"

"Could I...come and visit you? We could talk..."

Gretchen fell silent.

"Please...," the woman begged.

"All right," Gretchen said, as her emotions shifted between caution, terror, and a compelling desire to see this woman; to look into her eyes and search for the bond they must have once shared. "When do you want to come?"

"I could get a flight to L.A. this weekend. On Saturday."

This is a bad time, Gretchen thought, with Sam getting laid off. Still, the time might not be better for a while. She considered the family's plans for the weekend. Julia had a birthday party. That was all.

"Okay," Gretchen agreed. "Saturday. Call me with the flight information, and we'll be there to pick you up."

Chapter Six

Gretchen hung up the phone, shaken. She checked on the kids, needing to be reassured by their presence. Julia watched The Wizard of Oz with rapt attention. Bucky was in his room, playing with cars.

She roamed aimlessly through the house, picking dirty clothes off the floor. Her thoughts rambled. Her mother. She had barely thought of her in years. Now, the phrase entered her mind constantly, compulsively. Like an invasion. Like a compelling image.

She carried toys from the den to Bucky's room. The mess in her house was like a living thing, mole-like. It popped up in various rooms in the form of cluttered toys, books and dirty clothes, despite her efforts to contain it.

She could not keep ahead of the laundry. She managed to wash the clothes, but putting them away was another matter. Her king-sized bed was continually buried beneath a pile of clean laundry, which she and Sam routinely slept under, to Sam's chagrin. She had given up on a hamper–she kept the dirty laundry in a large, blue plastic trash can. When it was not overflowing, she kept the lid on.

She found the demands of a mother and homemaker endless, overwhelming. Because of her lack of a role model, she often felt bewildered.

She and Sam met when she was twenty-four, in a travel agency in San Diego where she had worked for a year. She had attended a junior college in Oklahoma for two years, then worked in the base commissary for a while. She had found the job in San Diego through a friend. Her father had remarried, and Ted had recently enlisted in the Air Force.

Sam had booked a flight to L.A., where he had an interview with Titan Technologies. He had called her. After landing the job, he commuted to San Diego on weekends to see her. Three months later, she had gotten pregnant, and Sam had asked her to marry him. She had moved into his apartment in Santa Monica, and hadn't worked outside the house since. She loved her children with a fierce devotion, and couldn't imagine leaving them for long hours every day while she went to work. Sam wanted her to be with the kids, and with his rising career, they had done well.

At first, she had not known what he expected of her. One night he said, while rummaging through the refrigerator, "Do you think maybe you could go out there, somewhere, buy some food and bring it home and cook it?"

"I guess," she had answered, shocked. Her father and Ted had foraged for themselves. She had never thought much about cooking. She checked out cookbooks from the library, and with some experimentation had become a fair cook.

The house, she simply couldn't keep up with. Now she looked forward to the new housekeeper coming Thursday. Especially since her mother would be arriving Saturday.

Gretchen dressed the kids warmly. The sky had cleared, but the weather remained cool. She put on a warm knit suit, and jeweled blue tennis shoes. On some days she favored knits, leather flats and thin gold bracelets. Other days, she wore her jeans, cowboy boots, and a leather belt with a silver-and-turquoise buckle and the word "Gretchen" carved across the back.

On the way to the park, Julia asked, "Are Dorothy's bones in the tar pits?"

Gretchen turned down the radio. "No, sugar. When people die they get buried under the ground." God, then there was cremation, which she couldn't possibly mention.

Julia seemed to be thinking, but asked no more questions.

❊ ❊ ❊

"What a cute little boy," the big, rangy woman with straight, dark-brown hair said. Gretchen assumed she must be the mother of the little girl Bucky had been scampering up and down the jungle gym with, a round-faced, cherubic child who squealed each time she went down the slide.

"Thanks," Gretchen said. "That's my daughter over there, playing with the bucket and shovel."

"What's your son's name?"

"Bucky."

"What?"

Gretchen laughed. "His real name is Buchanan."

"What a distinguished name."

Gretchen kept a close eye on Bucky as he slid down a pole. "Yeah. My husband insisted on naming him after his Grandfather Buchanan. I didn't have much say about it."

The woman nodded. "That must have been hard for you."

Gretchen wondered if she had misunderstood her, but before she could ask, the woman said, "Where are you from? The south?"

"Well, Oklahoma." She extended her hand. "I'm Gretchen."

"Terry," the woman said, grasping Gretchen's hand. "My daughter's name is Holly. The kids seem to be playing together well. Why don't we go sit on that bench?"

"Great," Gretchen agreed, following her to a green bench on the rim of the sandy play area.

"Do you think you'll have any more kids?" Terry asked after a while, eying Bucky and Julia.

"My husband says that if I get pregnant again...he'll kill himself."

Terry laughed. "I see. Well, two's a good number. Gretchen doesn't strike me as an Oklahoma name. I would have thought Becky Sue, or Tammy. Something like that."

"Oh, I wasn't born in Oklahoma. Actually, I was born in California. At Edwards Air Force Base, near Palmdale. My dad was in the Air Force, so until I was ten we lived in Colorado and Okinawa."

"What unique experiences."

"Yes," Gretchen said shyly, not used to so many questions from a stranger.

"What do you do now?" Terry asked.

"What do I do?"

"What kind of work do you do?"

"Well...I used to work in a travel agency. Now I'm home with my kids." Gretchen checked Terry's expression, wondering if she looked down on women who stayed at home.

"That's a big job," Terry said. She appeared to be in her mid-thirties. Even though she wore casual cotton slacks and a sweater, her makeup had been expertly applied, and the gold watch she wore seemed expensive. Gretchen was surprised to note that she didn't wear a wedding band.

Terry brought two cans of juice from her bag and offered Gretchen one. "How do you like living in Los Angeles?" she asked.

"It's okay." Gretchen smiled wryly, accepting the juice.

"How long have you been here?"

"Five years. It's a big city. Too big for me, I think sometimes. My husband Sam and I moved here when he got a job."

"So you probably don't have any other family here?"

"My dad lives in Oklahoma City. Del City, actually. He's retired from the Air Force and civil service. He lives in a mobile home now. My brother's in the service. He's stationed in Colorado." She couldn't think about Howard and Ted without missing them terribly. She and Sam had flown back with the kids over Christmas, and Ted had been on holiday leave.

"What about your mother?"

Gretchen started laughing, almost hysterically. The question seemed so timely, so pointedly absurd. She laughed, tears coming to her eyes. Tension drained out until she sat shaking, exhausted. And more relaxed than she had been in days.

"Wow! I didn't mean to hit a nerve."

"I don't know what's come over me," Gretchen coughed. Terry handed her a tissue. She wiped her eyes and sipped her juice.

"I mentioned your mother..."

"I know! See, until a few days ago, I thought she was dead. She left when I was twelve, and I never heard a word, all these years. The other day I got a letter. I called her, and she's coming this Saturday."

"My God," Terry said, pushing her brown hair over one ear and shifting on the bench. "That's incredible."

"Yeah," Gretchen agreed. "Getting the letter was a shock. I don't know...what to think yet. I guess Saturday will be a pretty big day."

"What an opportunity," Terry said. "Excuse me." She ran into the sandy play area and kneeled down beside Bucky and Holly. The two children pulled on each end of a small blue shovel, howling.

"You have to share, Bucky!" Julia said, appearing next to the smaller children.

"Why don't you offer this to your brother," Terry said, taking out a red shovel from her bag and handing it to Julia. Bucky let go of the blue shovel and grabbed the red one from Julia.

"What a good helper you are," Gretchen heard Terry say to Julia. Julia gave her a cockeyed, suspicious smile.

When Terry returned to the bench, Gretchen asked, "What do you mean? About meeting my mother being an opportunity?"

Terry sat back and shoved her hands into the pockets of her slacks. Her eyes remained on the children. "Maybe you'll have a second chance. To resolve your relationship with your mother."

"Well...maybe," Gretchen said thoughtfully.

"You know, lots of people are estranged from their parents, and have just given up." She smiled at Gretchen, in a big-sisterly way. Her eyes crinkled. "Maybe you'll work it out."

"That could take a miracle," Gretchen said. "I don't even know her."

"Miracles happen."

"And to make things worse, my husband just got laid off," she said suddenly, amazed by how much she had revealed to this woman. Yet, it felt good to talk.

"Laid off?" Terry shook her head. "You're getting hit from all sides. What does he do?"

"He...he's in the defense industry," Gretchen answered cautiously, lest Terry be offended by Sam's line of work.

"That's a sad situation," Terry said. She crossed her legs, swinging her foot. "So many families are going to get hurt by these defense cuts, and bases closing."

"I know!" Gretchen said, grateful that Terry understood. "I'm glad we're not at war with Russia anymore...well, at odds, that is. Of course I'm glad. But still..."

"For once," Terry said, apparently lost in her own train of thought, "Not having to worry so much about a nuclear war, even an accidental one. I remember as a kid, during the Cuban Missile Crisis, when we had all those drop drills at school." She gazed at her daughter, who sat in the sand with legs outstretched, intent on her digging. "For the first time in my life, I'm hopeful our children won't have to live under the constant threat of nuclear war. It's...exhilarating."

"Yes, it is," Gretchen said, agonized, the sky a gray shield behind her. "But I don't know what we're going to do."

Terry seemed to consider Gretchen's plight. "Your husband will probably get another job, won't he?"

Gretchen released her breath in a heavy whoosh. "He wants to start his own business. He seems so confident, but I don't know. I wish he still had his job, or one just as secure."

"You must be scared," Terry said after a moment.

"Damn right I'm scared," Gretchen said, her eyes hard and glinting. "I don't ever want to live like..."

"Like?"

"Like we did in Oklahoma, on the base," Gretchen finished quietly. "My dad was enlisted. Just being enlisted, you're second-class. He insisted on saving any extra for college for me and my brother, Ted. Then when his mother got sick, we had to put her in a nursing home until she died. We were poor. I don't ever want to be poor again," she said fiercely.

"I suppose your father was in the service before Reagan started dumping money into the military," Terry said. She reached into her diaper bag and drew out a brush and a pink ponytail band.

Gretchen nodded. The day had warmed. She pushed up the sleeves of her knit shirt. "Most enlisted men worked second jobs to make ends meet. But after my mother took off, he had to stay with me and Ted."

"So, did he remarry?" Terry asked. She swept her hair up behind her head and fastened the band around it. Short wisps of dark hair remained around her ears.

"He married Mary Ann a few years ago. She's really great."

"You like her, then?"

"Yeah, I do. I don't have to take care...worry about him anymore."

"Oh, so you took care of him after your mother left?" Terry said, more of a statement than a question.

Gretchen lowered her eyes. "I guess. What else could I do?"

"What else?"

In sudden silence, the women watched their children playing.

"Do you work?" Gretchen asked curiously, her eyes on Bucky and Holly. The children jumped up and down on the suspended wooden bridge. Julia sat under the slide with another little girl, digging a hole.

"I'm a Jungian analyst."

"What's that?"

Terry laughed. "Oh, I'm just a therapist. A counselor. But I studied the teachings of Carl Jung, an associate of Sigmund Freud who developed his own philosophy. I have a private practice in the evenings, so I can be with Holly during the day. That's important to me, too."

A therapist. No wonder Terry had been so...understanding. For a moment she felt exposed, even tricked. She hated the idea of psychologists picking people apart. Privy to innermost, personal secrets. She couldn't imagine talking to a counselor herself. But she looked at Terry's face, and saw no malice, no hint of exploitation. Only friendliness and sincerity.

"So you just talk to people?" Gretchen asked.

"Well, I do dream analysis, too. Jung was big on dreams and symbols. Like Freud, he believed strongly in the unconscious. In particular, the collective unconscious."

"The collective unconscious?"

"Sure. That's the concept that ideas, if you will, can surface from the unconscious to various groups who are not necessarily in the same place. For instance, the women's movement, in the 1960s, didn't arise only in the United States, but all around the world. Another example is a case in which monkeys on an island began washing their fruit in the ocean before eating it, and the same phenomenon began to occur with monkeys in other parts of the world. Why? The collective unconscious, perhaps."

Gretchen had taken a psychology class in junior college, and vaguely remembered Jung and Freud and the unconscious.

"Are you...married?" Gretchen asked. She didn't want to intrude, but was curious about Terry's missing wedding ring.

Terry gazed over at Holly. "I was. But John left me."

"How long ago was that?"

"Six months after Holly was born," Terry said sadly. "He felt threatened by my career. Oh, I make enough money to support myself and Holly, but...well, it's been hard. I liked being part of a couple. I hate being lonely."

"I'm sorry," Gretchen said lamely. For all my troubles, she thought, Sam and I are stable.

"Look," Terry said. "I come here most Monday mornings. Why don't we meet again? I really like talking to you. I have a feeling we're going to be friends."

Pleased, Gretchen agreed. She felt less alone, less panicked.

Later, when Gretchen drove home from the park with Julia and Bucky tired and dirty in the back seat, she felt calmer, and strangely resigned. Saturday loomed ahead, and her reunion with her mother.

But for once in her life, the future held the possibility of something separate from Sam, from her father or her children. A friendship with Terry. A new relationship with her mother.

In spite of Sam's layoff, the future suddenly teemed with opportunities. She drove home, her hands steady on the wheel, her mind brimming with hope.

Chapter Seven

When the doorbell rang at eight o'clock Thursday morning, Gretchen had already been cleaning her house for over an hour.

"What are you doing?" Sam had asked before he left for work. He and the children watched her scurrying from room to room with armloads of toys, books and clothes.

"I don't want the new housekeeper to think I'm a complete slob," Gretchen had answered distractedly, stooping again and again to pick up toys and socks from the floor. She wore a pink-flowered, flannel nightgown, and her feet were bare.

"I've never seen you so...motivated," Sam had remarked as he walked out the door to take Julia to school and go to work, but she barely heard him.

The woman stood on the front step, an old upright vacuum cleaner and a cardboard box full of cleaning supplies at her feet. Moon-faced, she grinned at Gretchen with gold-filled teeth. Her black hair, laced with white, hung to her shoulders. Short and stocky in her faded blue dress, she might have been thirty. Or forty.

"You are Mrs. Carey?" she asked, her English distinct despite a heavy Spanish accent. "I am Rósa."

"Come in," Gretchen said, a little nervously. She held the door open wide. "I'm so glad you're here. Like I told the agency, I guess I need some help around here. Actually," she laughed self-consciously, "I'm not a very good housekeeper. My husband would like the house a bit neater, and I can't really keep up with it."

The woman nodded, carrying her supplies through the door.

"I've never had a housekeeper here before," Gretchen said, twisting her fingers together. "Do you want me to show you where to start? I tried to pick up most of the toys, to make it easier for you to clean."

"Okay," Rósa said agreeably. "I start in the bathrooms, then the kitchen. But whatever you like, you tell me."

Gretchen took a deep breath. "Follow me down the hall. I'll show you where the first bathroom is."

Bucky stood in the middle of the hall, in a T-shirt and diaper, clutching his tattered white blanket to his chest.

Rósa's face lit up. "Hello," she said gently, squatting to Bucky's level. Her finger stroked his chin, and he giggled. "How are you?"

"He's our baby," Gretchen explained, delighted that Rósa seemed taken with him. "Our daughter is four. She's in preschool today."

"What is your name?" Rósa asked, and Bucky pulled his blanket over his head.

The women laughed.

"This is Bucky. Do you have children?"

Rósa nodded. "Two children." She held up two fingers. "They live in El Salvador."

"Oh, are they grown, then?"

"No. My daughter, she is five. My son is seven."

Puzzled, Gretchen asked, "Why aren't they here with you?"

Rósa straightened up. Bucky gave her his silly grin. "I come here to earn money. I send it back to my family."

"But why can't your children live with you?"

Rósa shrugged. "I have no way to support them here. America is very...expensive."

"When will you see them again?"

"I don't know," Rósa said calmly. "It is...difficult. The war is very bad. We have no money."

Gretchen had heard about civil wars in Central American countries for years. El Salvador, Nicaragua, Argentina. She barely knew the difference, and certainly not the issues.

"What about your husband?" Gretchen asked.

Rósa picked up her box of cleansers, moving past Bucky toward the bathroom. "My husband fights in the war," she replied. "My children live with my sister."

While Rósa started work, Gretchen dressed Bucky and took him out to the backyard to play on the swing set. Shortly, she would take him to the grocery store and to pick up Sam's pants at the cleaners.

As she rhythmically pushed Bucky on the swing, she pondered her uneasiness about Rósa. How could any mother leave her children alone in a country ravaged by war? Then bitterly, she realized that of course a mother could abandon her children. She had first-hand experience. As she pictured Rósa's small children, who had no knowledge of when they might see their own mother again, she felt doubly pained. To abandon her own children would be unimaginable, an act she felt incapable of. How could any mother, her own or Rósa, do such a thing? She pushed Bucky, the chill morning air stinging her face, lost for answers.

Later, as she prepared to leave for the store with Bucky, she found Rósa in the kitchen. The bathrooms had been scrubbed spotless and smelled of lemon soap. Clearly, Rósa knew her trade. Now the woman stood on a stool, cleaning cupboards and rearranging cans and boxes in meticulous order. Gretchen watched her for a moment. I wish I could be so efficient, she thought.

"You like?" Rósa asked, smiling, a moist cloth in her hand.

"Yeah, it's great! I guess you've been doing this for a long time."

"Two years."

"That's how long you've lived in the United States?" Gretchen asked. She thought again of Rósa's children, without their mother all this time.

"Yes," Rósa answered. She climbed down from the stool. She set it down in front of another tall cupboard, and began to remove the contents to the counter.

"What did you do in...El Salvador?" Gretchen asked curiously.

Rósa faced her squarely. "I was a teacher."

Gretchen lowered her eyes. "I see," she said. Her own recent troubles seemed to fade. She watched Rósa work for a few more moments. Shoulders back, her brown face gleaming with moisture, bearing her loss like a soldier in war.

"How does your mouth feel now?" Gretchen asked as she and Sam lay in bed that night.

"Like tofu. The worst thing about a root canal is the novocaine."

"My...mother left a message on the machine. She's coming Saturday, at four o'clock."

"Oh," he said sleepily. "We can take her out to dinner."

Gretchen blinked, amazed at how he made this impending, cataclysmic event sound like a typical Saturday night.

"The housekeeper did a good job," Sam said, and she felt relieved to change the subject.

"She's from El Salvador. At first I thought she was from Mexico," Gretchen said. She inched toward him in bed and lay her head on his shoulder.

"What made you think that?" Sam asked. He had worked most of the evening on his fuzzy logic program. His current progress momentarily staved off her fear of losing everything.

"I thought all these women were from Mexico. You know, housekeepers."

He stroked her forehead. Her jaw grew slack, relaxing. "More women are coming to the United States from Central America."

"Why?"

"Rósa's from El Salvador? The civil war down there has plundered the economy for ten years. There aren't any jobs. There's no way to make a living. Women like Rósa come here to work as domestics, then send money home. American dollars go a long way in El Salvador."

"I don't see how she could leave her children."

He pushed her hair off her forehead and she drifted with the sensation. "Motherhood is different in El Salvador. People don't get married and plan a family like they do in the United States."

"What do you mean?"

"I mean that El Salvador has been turned upside down by war. Young women get raped by an uncle, or a soldier, or even a family friend and have a child."

"Jesus!"

"I'm sure the mothers love their children. But usually a grandmother or an aunt cares for these kids while the mothers work. I don't think there's the same kind of attachment, say, that you have for Bucky and Julia."

Gretchen thought of Rósa and the two children left behind, and wondered how that could be possible.

Sleepily, she remembered summer evenings, the weekend approaching, when she had returned to Woodland Hills from a shopping trip, or from the park with the kids. She had eased the white Volvo along the winding boulevards, a silvery line of expensive cars behind her, as a trail of brown-skinned women trudged slowly down along the side of the road on their way to meet the bus.

❄ ❄ ❄

Sometime in the early morning, Julia approached the foot of their bed. "Mommy," she whispered urgently. "I had a nightmare. Can I come in your bed?"

Gretchen pulled back the covers and her daughter crawled in next to her. Julia's breathing became deep and regular after a few moments. Gretchen turned on her side, watching Julia's face. She fell asleep easily, comforted by the presence of her daughter, and the love that filled her like soft warm light.

Chapter Eight

Saturday afternoon, as Gretchen rode with Sam and the children to pick up her mother at the airport, she braced herself in her seat with both legs as if she were afraid the car brakes would fail.

Sam glanced at her. "Are you okay? You seem a little tense."

Tense? The word hardly described how she felt. Petrified, maybe. Or terrified. She felt so tense she could float out the window. She gripped her seat. Sam is driving too fast, she thought. I'm not ready...to meet her.

Sam took one hand off the steering wheel and flipped down the visor for his sunglasses. "Man, I'm tired," he said, his voice bringing her down a little. "What time did Julia get into bed with us last night?"

"One o'clock, maybe two. She's been having bad dreams, Sam. Lots of kids go through that."

"I know, but she kicks me and pummels me bloody. She jabbed me all night in the head with her elbow. I barely got any sleep."

"Really? I didn't notice."

"She's over on my side of the bed!" He glanced over his shoulder, then changed lanes to exit off the freeway. "Nice signal, buddy," he said, referring to the car ahead of them. His eyes, behind his dark green glasses, were indiscernible.

"You're just a little tired, Sam," Gretchen said. "Maybe you should try to get some rest tomorrow." But she didn't know what tomorrow would be like anymore. Tomorrow a woman who claimed to be her mother would be in her house. What would the family do, or say, tomorrow?

"We're going to get Grandma, Mommy?" Julia asked.

"I wish you hadn't told her that, Sam."

"What was I supposed to tell her?" Sam snapped. "Do you think you can keep this...situation from her?"

"This isn't Grandma Carey, honey," Sam said, turning his head toward the back seat. "This is Mommy's mommy."

"My Granma," Bucky said solemnly.

Julia frowned. "I don't remember this Grandma."

"I don't remember her either," Gretchen said. The car sped toward her ambivalent reunion, the blood pulsing in her ears like a stopwatch.

❄ ❄ ❄

"How do we know what she even looks like?" Sam asked. The plane arriving from Dallas had been announced minutes earlier, and passengers began straggling up the ramp.

"In the phone message, she said she'd be wearing a bright yellow suit," Gretchen said. She gripped Sam's arm, her knees so weak she thought she would stagger. Her eyes never wavered from the ramp except to check her children. Julia and Bucky watched with rapt fascination through the slanted window as the planes took off into the sky. Each time a passenger arrived, beaming happily at waiting relatives, she flinched with relief. Then anxiously, she searched the face of the next person.

I can't stand it anymore, Gretchen thought. Then a woman with short, curly brown hair, wearing a bright yellow suit, stood at the top of the ramp. Gretchen thought she would faint.

The woman gazed around for a few moments, looking scared, and then her eyes found Gretchen's face. If Gretchen had ever doubted that a mother would recognize her own child, the woman dispelled those thoughts as her eyes locked with Gretchen's.

"Come on, that must be her," Sam said as he pulled Gretchen toward the woman.

Gretchen stumbled, suddenly dizzy, caught between a desire to run to the woman who was her mother, yet run away.

Sam continued to drag her, and then she was standing face to face with her mother. The woman clutched her black pocketbook against her chest like a shield. Her eyes glittered as her gaze drifted from Sam and Gretchen to the children. Her smile seemed frozen on her face, and Gretchen could swear she was trembling. Then Gretchen caught the smell of bourbon on her breath. A part of her seemed to close up. She remembered the feeling–like she had been let down yet again–and realized with a shock that she had experienced that same disappointment before, years ago, with her mother.

She reached for Sam's arm. She turned hurt eyes to his face, but he was smiling, extending his hand. The children crowded against her legs, staring. For a moment she felt on the outside of a closed circle.

"I'm Sam, and this is Julia and Bucky. Buchanan. I hope you had a good flight."

"Well, I hate to fly." Her mother's voice was raspy, her accent heavier than her own. "I always have to have something to drink. It helps me..."

Her mother took Sam's hand, dropping her pocketbook. Everyone reached for the purse on the floor, bumping heads. She straightened up, clearly flustered, and turned to Gretchen with moist brown eyes.

"Sugar," she said, her voice quivering. "You've grown up so beautiful. Like I knew you would."

"Mom," Gretchen managed to say, and it was as if she were twelve years old again.

Her mother embraced her and lay her cheek next to her own, cool and moist with tears. The familiarity of her mother's body, the thin shoulders and soft breast, stirred the memories and feelings of her lost childhood. She pulled away and stared at Sam's face. For an instant she felt strangely caught between two places in time, not quite recognizing either one.

"You...haven't changed that much," Gretchen said kindly. True, her mother's face resembled her picture in the old photo. Yet, she had aged so much. The firm, vibrant skin she remembered now appeared slack, wrinkled. She stared at the thick mascara, the blue eye shadow, the bold red mouth.

"My goodness." Carole gazed back sharply at Gretchen's face.

"I've wondered all these years what you sounded like. It should have occurred to me. You sound just like...Oklahoma."

"I don't remember what you sounded like," Gretchen said. "But you sound kind of like Texas, yourself. Is that where you've lived all these years?" The question, loaded like a firecracker, came out sounding casual.

"That's right, I have." Carole fumbled in her handbag, then brought out a pack of cigarettes and a lighter. Her hands shook as she drew out a cigarette, put it to her mouth and lit it.

Gretchen and Sam exchanged a glance. "Well, should we get going?" Sam asked finally.

Bucky and Julia stared up at Carole. Her weathered face broke into a smile. She bent down to the children's level. "My grandchildren. You don't know how much I've been looking forward to meeting you. Here, I brought something for you." She reached into a soft bag at her feet and brought out a baby doll for Julia, and a little red truck for Bucky. Greedily, the children grabbed their presents.

"She looks just like you," Carole said, and Gretchen smiled at her, her pride taking over.

"Come on! Let's pick up your luggage and get out of here," Sam said, and guided the family toward the escalator.

❄ ❄ ❄

When they arrived home after dinner, Gretchen showed Carole through the house. "This room is for you," she said, as Sam placed her bags in the spare bedroom.

"My God, what a beautiful room," Carole remarked, taking in the satin curtains, the large Chinese area rug and the four-poster bed covered with handmade quilts. Then her eyes stopped at the oak cabinet. Gretchen's guns hung in clear view through the glass.

"I see he gave those to you," Carole remarked.

"My guns? Yes, he did. You remember them, then?"

"I remember everything about him," she said quietly, her voice venomous. "And about Oklahoma."

The force of her bitterness shocked Gretchen. She had always thought of her father as blameless. He was a good man, and her mother had run out on the family.

"Do you mind if I rest for a few minutes?" her mother asked, sitting on the bed. "I'm afraid I tire easily these days."

"Of course," Gretchen said, disappointed. If only she and her mother could talk. Dinner had been impossible. The kids had been excited, chattering constantly, wanting their grandmother's attention every minute.

She found Sam and the children at the dining room table. Julia, thick crayon in hand, made careful strokes in a coloring book. Bucky sat on Sam's lap, scribbling wildly in his book.

"She wants to rest for a while," Gretchen said, sitting across from him.

"No wonder."

"What's that supposed to mean?"

"Jesus, Gretchen. Did you see her belt down those two bourbon and sodas at dinner? Who knows how many she had on the plane? I'm surprised she didn't pass out."

"Yes," Gretchen admitted. She combed her hair with her fingers, longing for order in her self, in her life. Somehow, she had imagined this reunion with her mother would be sweet and poignant. The reality of this imperfect meeting left her feeling bruised and despairing.

"Do you...like her?" Gretchen asked.

Sam seemed to gather his thoughts. "She's a little coarse, and I wonder about her drinking. But she's trying, I can tell you that. I think we should give her a chance, honey. I know you're angry and upset with her. But give her a little time, okay?"

"I'll try, Sam," Gretchen said, toying with a crayon. "I just thought it might be different." She looked up at him, and he gave her a questioning glance. "I thought...I hoped," her voice came out low, strained, as she searched for words. "I didn't expect her to be so old, so washed out. And how could she–how could she drink like that, on her way to meet me?" She choked back the hurt, and suddenly the crayon broke in her fingers. "What does she want, anyway?"

"Maybe she can't help it," Sam mumbled after a moment, rubbing her arm in a consoling gesture.

Her mother was a stranger. Suddenly, she wished Carole had never contacted her, never invaded her life.

She and Sam moved stiffly through the next hour, like ghosts in their own home. They played with the children and put them to bed. Speaking in low voices, their privacy seemed transparent because of the woman behind the closed bedroom door.

❊ ❊ ❊

After Sam and the children went to bed, Gretchen stayed up, idly sorting through the day's mail at the dining room table. She checked her watch. Nine-thirty.

"I got a nice little nap," her mother said, appearing in the room. She stretched her shoulders and yawned.

"I expected you would be sleeping through the night," Gretchen said in surprise.

Her mother smiled and sat across from her. "I thought so too, but now I'm wide awake." Her expression reflected the fragile, amicable mood, as if she wanted to tread carefully. "Sam seems like an awfully nice man," she said.

"Oh, he is," Gretchen said proudly. "I've never known a better man than Sam. Except for Dad, of course." She raised her head, her stare slightly challenging.

"Well, what does he do, anyway?" her mother asked.

Gretchen hesitated, hating to be reminded of Sam's work and his impending layoff.

"He...works in defense, Mother."

"My, so that's why you're living so well. That's wonderful," she said enthusiastically. "That field is so secure. Is he in civil service?"

Irritated, Gretchen tossed the mail on the table. "No, Mother. He works for a company that makes bombs. And now that the Cold War is over, his boss is giving it all up for garbage."

"I don't understand," her mother said in a hurt voice.

"I mean he's getting laid off next week. We're at peace with Russia now. We don't need to make any more bombs. Sam's company is getting into garbage recycling."

"Oh, sugar. I'm sorry."

"You called me that when I was a little girl, didn't you?"

"I did," Carole said, and the awkwardness hung between them like a wedge. Gretchen had once been loved by this stranger, who had abandoned her without a backward glance.

Gretchen squared her shoulders. "Don't worry about Sam. He's starting his own business. He's sure it will be a big success."

"Of course it will! He looks like a man who can succeed at anything he puts his mind to."

"Yes, he does, doesn't he," Gretchen said, pleased that her mother saw Sam's best quality.

After a moment Carole asked, "Do you have any brandy?"

Gretchen gave her a long, cool look, then said, "Sure. I'll get it for you." She returned with a small tumbler, half full.

"How long have you lived in Texas?" Gretchen asked.

"Oh, about seventeen years now," her mother answered vaguely.

"Since I was twelve, and you left?"

"I guess that's right." Carole sipped her brandy. The light filtered through the amber liquid and she stared at it, as if mesmerized.

Furious at her seeming lack of interest, Gretchen lashed out. "Did you ever think about writing to us? Or did you think we'd forget you, like you forgot us?"

"I did write to you! For ten years."

"I don't believe you! I never got any letters!" Gretchen said, astonished.

"Why do you think you didn't get them?" her mother asked bitterly.

"Dad?" Gretchen said in horror. "He would never do that!"

"Wouldn't he?" Carole took another slug, then stared deep into the glass as if the bottom contained her memories.

Gretchen knew her mother was telling the truth. "He said you never wrote. He even acted like he was sorry."

Carole's gaze remained steady, conveying her position on the matter.

"But why did you leave us?" Gretchen persisted.

Her mother sighed. "Let me get a cigarette," she said.

"Please don't smoke in the house."

"Can we go outside, then?"

"All right." Several minutes later they sat at the round white table in the back patio, wrapped in coats. The air had warmed over the last few days, but remained damp and penetrating. A dome of clouds hung low in the sky, illuminated by a full moon. A dog barked lazily several houses away. In the distance she could hear loud music and laughter, strange for this neighborhood.

Her mother inhaled deeply, then coughed spasmodically. "I hated Oklahoma," she said finally.

"That's it?" Gretchen asked, incredulous.

Carole's eyes darted away from Gretchen's accusing stare. "Well, it was so long ago, sugar. Your father and I were...unhappy. It wasn't just Oklahoma. It was the Air Force, as well. When I married your father, he planned to finish school, become an officer. He never did. He stayed enlisted, and we had so little money."

"You left because Dad didn't have enough rank? He worked very hard at what he did! What kind of woman are you, to leave your family because of...snobbery?" Her voice cut like a razor, edged with rage and contempt. "You know," she said sharply. "I think there's something you're not telling me."

Carole's face paled against the metallic sky. "Can't you just leave the past alone? What does it really matter? I've come back, and I want to know you and your family."

Abruptly, Gretchen pushed her chair back and stood up. "I don't think I want to know you. Maybe you should just go back to where you came from. Tomorrow."

Carole moaned like a wounded animal, and her body seemed to sink into her chair. "Please, sugar," she begged. "I can't leave yet."

"Why not?"

Carole raised her chin, her gaze calm and piercing. Gretchen wavered, unnerved.

"Because I'm going to die."

Chapter Nine

Slowly, Gretchen sank back into her chair. "What did you say?"

"I have cancer," Carole said calmly. "I don't have much time left."

"That's why you're here, isn't it?" Even in the harsh glow of the porch light, Gretchen could see how pale, how thin her mother looked. The cough. The shaking hands. How had she not realized Carole was ill?

"I found out a month ago. I might have six months left, if I'm lucky," Carole said, her eyes brave but her voice betraying her fear.

"I'm sorry," Gretchen said softly. Yet, she might have been reacting with the same sympathy she would feel for a stranger. Not for a mother. Her mother was a stranger.

"After so many years of trying to contact you, I gave up. I could never stop loving you and Ted...but I hated myself, you see. I honestly believed you were better off without me."

Gretchen leaned forward in her chair. "But why...?"

Carole stared at her lap, her chin quivering. "I had to see you again. I had to get to know my grandchildren. To try and make...peace with you. Can you blame me for that?"

Gretchen held out her hand. Carole gripped it, smiling through tears.

"No, I can't. I'm sorry I was so mean."

"I can't blame you."

Suddenly, impulsively, but with more certainty than she had ever known in her life, Gretchen said, "I want you to come live with us. I think you should be with your...family."

"You really want me?" her mother sounded surprised. "I don't want to be a burden to you..."

"There's no question," Gretchen said. I cared for my father and Ted for years, she thought, and I've seen other women care for their parents. Her drinking, my own resentments...I'll find a way to deal with that. Right now, I want to be with her. I'm sure Sam will agree.

She smiled reassuringly at Carole, trying to hide her sadness. Strangely, a mood of peace settled between the women, now that the future had been laid out and secured. They moved inside the house, and talked about their everyday lives as they began to get to know each other. Gretchen listened, answering her mother's questions about herself and Ted as best she could. When Carole went to bed she sat alone for a few minutes. Everything was settled. Under control. But for the first time in her life, she felt old.

Later, in the bedroom, Sam said, "I'm sorry, honey. This must be really hard on you."

"Not as hard as you might think, Sam. I don't love her. But I don't want her to die alone, either. And she wants to get to know her grandchildren. She deserves that, no matter what she's done."

"When is she coming to stay?"

"In two weeks. She's going to sell the furniture in her apartment. She says she doesn't have that much stuff."

"Does she...work in San Antonio, or something?"

"She's worked in a department store for years."

"Gretchen. I hope she has health insurance."

"She does, Sam. Don't worry about that."

"This is not the time for us to be taking on any big medical bills. There's no way we could do that."

"I know! Her company has very good health insurance. I may not know much about her, but I don't think she would impose her medical bills on us."

"God, how is this going to affect the kids?" Sam lay on his back, staring at the ceiling.

"I guess they're going to learn a lot about real life. And death. People die. Years ago, it was common to keep a dying family member at home."

"That's all Julia needs. More death."

Suddenly, to her surprise, she said in rage, "This is my mother!"

"I'm sorry," he said quickly. "You're right." Then, "Did she explain why she left you?"

"No." She turned on her side and smoothed her flannel nightgown over her knees. "She doesn't want to talk about it. I think something really bad happened to her, back then. I just have to be patient, and trust that someday she'll tell me."

Sam nodded. "When does she go back to Texas?"

"Monday. I thought tomorrow we'd go to Placerita Canyon for a picnic, or something. The weather should be warm enough."

"Is she...up to that?" Sam asked.

"I think so. She's not that sick yet, Sam. She's got a tumor in her chest, though. Her doctor wants her to start radiation as soon as possible."

"Any hope?"

"She says no."

Sam was quiet. She reflected for a while on the events that had taken over her life. Everything has changed, she thought. Everything is different.

❆ ❆ ❆

Monday morning, the doorbell rang at seven-thirty. Sam and Gretchen were finishing cereal with the children at the table. Carole still slept.

"That's weird," Sam said, as Gretchen went to open the door.

Paula, her next door neighbor, stood on the porch like a woman on a mission. She wore her daily uniform: skirted blue suit, white oxford shirt, light-blue paisley bow tie, and black pumps with gold-tipped toes. Her dark brown hair, cut in what she called her "functional do", fell straight to the collar. In one hand, she clutched a leather briefcase. In the other, her son Joey.

"Gretchen! It's not too early, is it?" Paula asked.

Before Gretchen could answer, she stepped into the foyer and started down the hall, dragging Joey behind her.

"Oh, hi, Paula," Sam said, casting a tedious, "here we go again" glance at Gretchen.

Paula set down her briefcase, let go of Joey's hand, and plunked down in the easy chair. Joey tottered over to Bucky, who sat in his booster chair at the table, Tasty O's dribbling down his chin.

Paula's eyes swept over the room, her gaze finally landing on the still-bound newspaper on the coffee table.

"Hi, Sam. How's the bomb business? Say, I see you haven't had a chance to read about the big news this morning," she said casually.

Sam and Gretchen waited. "What?" Sam asked. "An earthquake? Another serial killer?"

Paula laughed. "Nothing like that. Another coup for the plight of women, Sam. As a man of the nineties, you should be impressed."

"Come on, Paula. What are you talking about?" Sam's exasperation toward Paula leaked out in the tone of his voice.

Paula's eyes flashed mischievously. "They finally awarded a woman a Nobel Prize!"

Sam's lips twisted in skepticism.

"Really!" Gretchen exclaimed. "How wonderful."

"Yeah," Paula continued. "A genetic researcher. Her work involves trying to discover the genetic differences between men and women."

"Uh-huh," Sam said, his interest clearly perked.

"She managed to isolate a testosterone molecule. She found that testosterone, which is found in abundance in men, can be broken into three distinct compounds."

"That's incredible," Gretchen said.

"What three compounds?" Sam asked.

Paula cleared her throat. "She's calling them Lust-erone, No-sense-rone and Messy-rone. An incredible breakthrough in understanding the nature of men, don't you think, Sam?"

Paula laughed, a hoarse giggle. Sam sat stone-faced, then slowly spooned another bite of cereal into his mouth.

"That is funny, Paula," Gretchen said finally. Her eyes appealed to Sam for confirmation, but she didn't get any.

Sam glared at Paula, then gave Gretchen his suffering, "how much of this am I expected to take from this woman" look.

"Is there something we can do for you, Paula?" Sam asked, a touch of impatience in his voice.

Paula sighed. "Actually, there is. Gretchen, I'm afraid María isn't coming today. She called an hour ago and said she wasn't feeling well. So, I was wondering..."

Gretchen tensed, knowing full well what Paula was about to ask.

"...you're home all day. I'm hoping Joey can stay with you today."

Paula's presumptuousness irritated Gretchen. Did she imagine it, or did women who worked outside the home assume that she, as a full-time homemaker, had nothing to do? She was constantly being asked to baby-sit, house-sit, hold the key to let in a neighbor's carpet cleaner, or worse, be a sympathetic sounding board about sore feet, stress, problems with the boss and other maladies of the career world. Couldn't her friends and neighbors understand that being a homemaker and mother was a full-time job, and that she was always busy?

"Paula...this isn't a good day. My...my mother is here."

"Your mother? Dear, you don't have a mother."

"I didn't," Gretchen admitted, suddenly keenly aware of the strangeness of her mother's reappearance. "But now I do. And she's here."

Paula scrutinized Gretchen's face, then backed off. "Okay," she said in a sulking tone. "I guess I'll take the day off, then."

Sam, as if expecting a confrontation, jumped up from the table and said, "I'm going to take my shower now." He disappeared into the kitchen, carrying a stack of breakfast dishes.

Paula stared after him, slowly shaking her head. "Why is it that after the age of four, all men seem to do is keep getting taller?"

Gretchen smiled, though still irritated. "I can keep Joey until three. That's the best I can do. Then I have to take my mother to the airport."

"Oh, thank God," Paula said dramatically, and a little triumphantly, pressing her hand to her chest.

"We'll have a good day," Gretchen said, more to convince herself. She felt slightly suckered. But now that she had decided to keep Joey, she might as well make the best of it. At least, her kids liked playing with him.

"Of course you will," Paula nodded in agreement. Then her eyes swept over the room again, and into the dining room, where boxes of cereal stood open on the table near puddles of milk, and toys littered the floor. "Really, Gretchen. I have no idea why you don't get a housekeeper."

"I did! From that agency you recommended. Her name is Rósa and she's great. She's coming again Thursday."

"You're going to love the help," Paula said with approval. "I couldn't live without María. Say, what do you think of our new neighbors at the Rialto house?"

"I haven't really noticed."

"You haven't noticed the motorcycles and the noisy, late night parties? In the mornings I've seen beer cans scattered on the lawn. I wonder if Mr. Rialto realizes..."

"I did hear music and shouting Saturday night," Gretchen said. "So it was coming from the Rialto house. Do you think some single people are renting it?"

"No! That's the kicker. There's just a young couple and a little girl. At night they invite all their wild friends. Can you imagine?"

"No," Gretchen said. "I feel sorry for the little girl."

"Well," Paula said brightly. "I've got to run. Be a good boy, Joey, and play with Buckaroo. Thanks again, Gretchen. You really helped me in a jam." She leaned down to kiss her son, then rushed out the door.

"What are we going to do today, Mommy?" Julia asked.

"We're going to visit with...Grandma. Then later we'll take her to the airport."

"I wish I had someone to play with."

"You can play with Joey."

"He's a baby!" she said scornfully, and turned toward her room.

She could hear Sam's voice down the hall. "Julia, before you wake us up again at night, you'd better have *three* nightmares!"

He appeared after a few minutes dressed for work, his hair wet and combed back.

"I'm out the door," he said.

Gretchen put her arms around him. "I'm sorry, Sam. You look tired."

"I'm beat! When is that kid going to sleep in her own bed?"

Gretchen sighed. "She's probably affected by what's happening with us. Children are very...sensitive."

"Well, I'm losing whatever sensitivity I had." He kissed her. "I guess I'll see you later tonight, when you get back from the airport. Tell your mother goodbye for me. You okay?"

"Yes," she said, kissing him back. "And I will."

Chapter Ten

Later in the morning, Gretchen and Carole took the children outside for a walk. The sky had cleared, and the day promised to be warmer. Gretchen loved her street, even if Sam thought the neighbors were losers. Pine and eucalyptus trees stood thickly in front of the houses, like sentinels, shading and cooling even in the peak of summer. Jacarandas spread their soft, web-like leaves over the street, and in the spring their flowers covered the asphalt like wispy purple feathers.

There were no sidewalks. Brown pine needles edged the sides of the street, sending up a sweet, musty scent through all seasons. Blue plumbago, flowering in tiny, powder-blue blossoms, cascaded over rustic fences. Gnarly rose vines grew wild. Sometimes, on a clear day, a cool, salty breeze blew in over the hills from the ocean beyond.

"Are you sure you're up to this?" Gretchen asked as she and her mother watched the children search for bugs in a neighbor's rock bed. She didn't refer only to her mother's health–Gretchen had caught the stale smell of liquor on Carole's breath, presumably from a bottle she had brought with her, when Carole emerged from her room earlier. The watery eyes, the occasional stumble as they meandered up the street, the hesitancy when she spoke, all both concerned and repelled Gretchen.

"Oh, sure," Carole said, nestling into her beige jacket. "I don't have many symptoms yet, although my doctor says I will soon. I never would have known I was this sick, except for a routine chest x-ray." As if on cue, she drew a pack of cigarettes out of her pocket and lit up.

"Have you thought about quitting?" Gretchen asked, amazed that her mother still smoked.

Carole gave her a disbelieving glance. "You were never a smoker, I can tell. I'm glad. Of course I've thought about quitting." She took a long drag, her eyes squinting from the smoke. "But I'm an addict."

Gretchen watched as Carole exhaled a stream of smoke through her nose. How can this be my mother? she wondered in despair. Odors of smoke and alcohol seemed to exude from this woman. Odors that were vaguely familiar, like a fleeting, unpleasant memory.

After a few moments Gretchen asked, "Can't you have surgery, or chemotherapy?"

"The tumor's too close to my heart. And chemo doesn't work against this kind of cancer."

"Oh."

"When I come back here, I'll find another doctor. My insurance will pay for him," Carole said, a hint of defensiveness in her tone.

"I know," Gretchen said. At least her mother didn't want to be a burden.

The children continued down the side of the street, Joey and Bucky holding hands. Gretchen and Carole followed them slowly. Ahead, a little girl sat on a grassy spot outside the Rialto house, near the street.

The children stopped and stared down at her. She peered up at them, shading her eyes with her hand.

"Are you our new neighbor?" Gretchen asked cheerfully. The little girl smiled up at her and nodded, dimples appearing in her cheeks. Her hair, shiny and black, had been cut away from her face in a page boy.

"How old are you?" Julia asked.

She held up five fingers.

"What's your name?" Gretchen asked.

"Lorie."

As Gretchen regarded the striking child, she found Paula's description of motorcycles and late night parties hard to believe. Maybe this child could be a friend for Julia, she thought.

She heard a screen door slam, and a young woman in tight jeans and a blue flannel shirt hurried toward them. She held a cigarette near her leg, her hand cocked. Gretchen noted the woman's unsmiling face, discolored by old acne scars, and the way Lorie's blue eyes seemed to darken with resignation as the woman approached.

"Can I help you with something?" the woman asked curtly.

"We're your neighbors. We live four houses down, on the other side of the street," Gretchen said easily, though she understood the woman's tone, and her stance: hand on hip, face wary. You're not welcome. Leave us alone.

"Is she five?" Gretchen pointed at Lorie. "She says she's five." When the woman nodded, Gretchen went on. "Julia is four-and-a-half. Maybe she could play with Julia."

"Well, maybe. Come on, Lorie! I'm taking you over to Danny's. I've got to go to work soon."

Reluctantly, the child rose.

"Where do you work?" Gretchen asked.

"At the Buffalo House. In the lounge."

She pulled Lorie toward the house. "Bye, now."

"Nice little girl," Carole said, watching them go into the house. She seemed to be sobering up. "The mother seems kind of shifty."

"Yes, she does," Gretchen agreed. If Lorie hadn't appealed to her so much, she wouldn't even consider letting Julia play with her. And certainly, she couldn't let Julia play at Lorie's house, with the motorcycles, and the parties and beer. But perhaps the next time she saw Lorie, she would invite her over. If the mother didn't mind.

Hours later, as she took Carole to the airport, she felt relieved that the weekend was over.

"You don't know how much this visit meant to me," Carole said, her eyes moist, as she waited to board her plane.

"Mother..." Gretchen carefully drew Carole's thin figure into her arms. She overlooked the stale smell of smoke that clung to her hair. She momentarily forgot Carole's stubborn and infuriating reluctance to give her the information she so desperately wanted regarding her childhood. She simply held her mother, as imperfect and far from any childhood ideal she had ever imagined, and realized the beginning of a connection she had given up hope for long ago.

As she and the children watched Carole's plane taking off through the tall, filmy glass windows inside the airport, she longed to get home, to Sam and the issues at hand.

❊ ❊ ❊

By the end of the next week, Gretchen wondered if she would ever get used to Sam being at home.

"Sam?" Gretchen said one afternoon as he stared at his computer screen. "Are we going to look at the finances now?"

"I'll be there in a minute."

Twenty minutes later, he appeared at the table. She had never thought about Sam at work. Had he been like this, moody and preoccupied? When he came home, he had always been warm and easy to be with. Lately, she had been afraid to even talk to him. His coldness hurt. His presence in the house made her feel more lonely than when he had been gone every day.

"Let's see," Sam said, holding the checkbook register. "We've got ten thousand in savings. And the IRAs amount to about six thousand. That's pretty good."

"I know," Gretchen said, sipping a soda. "But the mortgage is twenty-two hundred a month. And with bills and food, I usually pay out another four thousand each month."

"I still have six weeks severance pay coming."

"Six weeks," Gretchen repeated. "What happens after that?"

"By that time, we should have a small business loan to tide us over until my product starts to sell."

Should have. Six weeks. The words rang in Gretchen's head.

"I'm coming along in my fuzzy logic program," Sam said, as if sensing her fear.

"When do you think you'll have it finished?"

"In a couple of months. I'm almost done with my business plan."

"Really?" she said, surprised.

Sam shrugged. "I worked on it my last couple of weeks at work. Norman really didn't have anything else for me. One of the guys had his own business once, and helped me write it."

"How can you be so sure you'll get this loan?" Gretchen asked, vocalizing her worst fear.

Sam pushed his hair back from his forehead in a nervous gesture. "Gretchen! You're going to have to have a little confidence in me."

"This isn't about *you,* Sam!" she said in frustration, suddenly impatient with his insecurities. "This is about our family. Our whole future is hanging on some...business plan!"

"I don't think you're seeing the big picture, Gretchen."

"No!" she said hotly. "I'm dealing with the *little* picture. I pay the bills now. I know how much we owe. I know how much food costs, and the kids' clothes, and gas for the cars. What are we going to do, Sam, if we don't have any money?"

"That's not going to happen," he said, but this time his voice lacked conviction, heightening her fear.

"It happened to me before, Sam, in Oklahoma."

"I know, honey. But that was a long time ago."

She stared past him. "I'll never forget that decrepit little house on base, with the stained carpets, and the roaches as big as mice. We barely had any money anyway, the three of us on Dad's salary. Then Grandma Simpson–"

"Yes, I remember about Grandma Simpson," he said impatiently.

Irritated, Gretchen continued anyway, the force of the memory surprising her. "It broke us when we had to put her in a nursing home. Until Dad got his second job, in a liquor store at night, we could barely buy food, let alone pay bills. I hated that...it was so humiliating! Having to beg off to the bill collectors, and not even able to buy things we needed."

"I'm sure that was tough on you," he said, his voice softer.

"We were poor, Sam. And there was nothing good about it. I've come too far to go through that again."

"I know," Sam said. "Give me a few more weeks. All I need is a few more weeks."

❄ ❄ ❄

Carole arrived and settled into the Carey household. To

Gretchen's vast relief, her mother assumed an undemanding, pleasant role in the house. She was kind and helpful with the children, and tactfully retired to her room when she sensed Sam and Gretchen wanted privacy. Sometimes she drank, usually in her room. Gretchen tried to ignore it, avoiding her if possible.

Now that Gretchen knew her mother was going to die, she began to regard her as someone surreal. A figure she had never known and never would know, who would soon vanish again. Although Gretchen hadn't attended church regularly in years, she found herself turning more to God and prayer.

One warm spring afternoon, shortly after Carole's arrival, Gretchen met Terry in the park.

"So, how's your mom?" Terry asked. Julia and Bucky were scrunched into a picnic bench beside Terry's daughter, Holly, eating ice cream from the truck. Terry had laid out a blanket on the grass, and the women nibbled raisins and carrot sticks while they talked. A warm breeze blew leaves across the blanket.

"All right, I guess," Gretchen shrugged. "What can I say? She's sick and she's a drunk. Sometimes I like her, and other times I hate her and wish she'd never shown up."

Terry was silent for a moment. "She's been an unexpected surprise, I know. I hope she'll open up and you can try to get some things resolved."

"I hope so too," Gretchen said, chewing on a blade of grass. "But I'm realistic, Terry. I'm always so realistic."

"Is she getting worse?" Terry asked after a minute.

"The radiation is making her weaker. Her chest hurts a little."

"I thought the radiation was supposed to help."

"I guess it is," Gretchen said. "After her treatments she's supposed to feel better for a while. She might even have a few extra months."

"Is she on pain medication?"

"Yeah, nothing that strong, though. She doesn't have much pain. It's more...her doctor that bothers me."

"You don't like him?"

"Not really." Gretchen shook her head. "She has radiation every day. Then she sees the doctor once a week. We always have to wait an hour to see him. I think the office books ten people for her same time slot. Then the doctor sort of...talks down to her."

Terry snorted. "That's how doctors are. Haven't you ever been sick?"

"Just minor stuff. I had the kids. I guess I had to wait a long time to see my doctor. Otherwise, I don't remember having any trouble."

"You're lucky. Doctors are so arrogant. I detest them." Then she asked, "How's Sam?"

"Fine, I suppose. It's strange having him in the house. He works most of the time on his computer in the study."

"He's making progress then? That's great!"

"He is." Gretchen sounded troubled. "He's going to submit his business plan next week, and hopefully we'll get a loan. But the money's going so fast, and I wish I had some sort of..."

"Guarantee?"

"Yeah."

Terry gave her a cynical smile. "I thought I had my life all wrapped up too, before John left me. What is it that the Buddhists say? Everything changes, nothing stays the same. Attachment is the root of all suffering."

"Is that what they say?" Gretchen asked, interested. "I never thought my life would change like this, though. Sam out of work, my mother here with me suddenly, dying. I thought my life would only change for the better. Shows how much I knew." She shaded her eyes and looked toward the ring of mountains, north of the valley. "God, it's smoggy today. Wouldn't it be wonderful if there wasn't any more smog?"

"The oil companies would never allow that!" Terry retorted.

"But think how great it would be if we didn't have pesticides in our food, or acid rain, or polluted water," Gretchen persisted.

"Impossible! The pesticide companies and oil industry would lose billions. So would our politicians. It will never happen."

"Maybe not," Gretchen said mildly, "But when I think of my children, I wish there was a way. I worry about the rainforests, and the animals being driven to extinction, especially the elephants."

Terry flashed her a humoring smile, then nibbled on the end of a carrot stick. "Why do you have such a thing about elephants?"

"They're magnificent," Gretchen said without hesitation.

"They live in families, and the babies and mothers are mowed down with machine guns by people who don't care. People who just cut off their tusks and leave them to rot. They're big and powerful, but so defenseless. They're almost prehistoric, like the mammoths. Elephants should always endure, and something is terribly wrong that they've almost been wiped out." She shaded her eyes and saw the children across the play area, washing their hands in a drinking fountain. "Sometimes I pray for the world."

"Do you actually go to church?"

"I did in Oklahoma. But Sam–he won't go. And I'm not all that wild about church, really. I still pray at home, though."

Terry smiled. "I like what Carl Jung said about religion."

"What?"

"Something about religion not being the absolute word of God, as the Christians believe, or complete nonsense, as atheists believe. But that religion developed out of man's dreams and symbols as he evolved. Religion arose from the subconscious, and reflects our quest for meaning and our fears and beliefs about death."

Gretchen snorted. "And you think Carl Jung is so smart? I think I'll keep praying."

"Do you remember what I once told you about the collective unconscious?" Terry asked. She lay back, leaning on her elbows, and watched the children running across the grass. "An idea that appears in different places in the world, at the same time?"

"I remember."

"I believe that someday all the peoples of the world will rise up and demand a stop to pollution, deforestation, overpopulation and the systematic extinction of animal species."

"You really think so?" Gretchen asked, intrigued.

"Yes, I do. Did you ever think in a million years that the United States and Russia would be on the same team, and for once we wouldn't have to live under the fear of nuclear war?"

"No," Gretchen said softly. "And I didn't think Sam would ever be out of work, either."

Terry seemed thoughtful for a few moments. "What if Sam finds work where he is actually making a contribution to the world? Don't you think that would be better than what he was doing before? Making weapons of annihilation?"

"Of course I do!" Gretchen said. "What a question." Bucky trotted across the blanket, and she wiped his face with a wet cloth. "But what kind of work? Right now he's trying to develop a computer program to improve car brakes."

"I know," Terry said. "But think about all the nuclear waste left behind after a decade of building bombs. What if Sam got into cleaning that mess up? That would be sort of a circular event in his life, don't you think? Wouldn't that be appropriate, after the big mess he helped to make?"

Gretchen resisted the urge to be defensive. Terry made no apology about being opposed to the United States' nuclear proliferation. She's right, Gretchen thought. Now that the years of nuclear gluttony are over, all that's left is a mess, and thousands of bombs to dismantle.

"We all have to figure out what we're supposed to do in life," Terry said. "So in my own way, I'll pray that it happens for Sam. And for you."

Chapter Eleven

❦❦❦

Can't we ask her to play?" Julia begged. Gretchen and Julia had come out in the front yard to pull weeds. The bright, soft warmth of the April sun had enticed Gretchen to be outside, away momentarily from the presence of her mother's illness in the house. Across the street, Lorie pedaled her pink bicycle, venturing further from her house and closer to the Carey's. She waved and Julia waved back, jumping up and down.

Gretchen balked. She did not have a good feeling about Lorie's family. In the weeks since she had first met Lorie, she often saw her mother and father, Lorie between them, going too fast down the street in a blue pickup truck. If she passed them in her car, or walked by their house, they averted their eyes when they saw her. The man scared Gretchen, with his shoulder-length, greasy hair and sleeveless shirts, his arms heavy like a laborer's. The constant presence of motorcycles, the loud music at night, and beer bottles frequently strewn across the lawn put her off as well.

"Please, Mommy!"

"All right," Gretchen said reluctantly. "Let's see if she can play."

Gretchen held Julia's hand crossing the street–not that it was busy, but because of habit–and approached Lorie, who had stopped her bike and straddled it with one foot on a pedal and one foot on the ground.

"My mom says we can play!" Julia said exuberantly.

"Is your mother home?" Gretchen asked, and Lorie nodded. Gretchen and Julia followed her to her house, then into the dirt driveway. The weeds had become overgrown in the front yard,

Gretchen noticed, and she saw several crushed beer cans lying near the porch.

Lorie opened the screen door while Gretchen and Julia waited silently outside. Gretchen peered through the screen. The house was dark inside, oppressive, and smelled of stale cigarette smoke.

Lorie returned with her mother. The woman wore a black halter top and white jeans. As before, she carried a cigarette in her hand.

She regarded Gretchen and Julia with wary, dark brown eyes. Lorie pulled at her hand.

"Lorie wants to come over and play?" she asked. "I don't know if you're busy..."

"No! We'd love to have her," Gretchen said quickly. "We've just been working in the garden."

"Okay...if you don't think she'll be any trouble." The woman had the slow, easy voice of a Californian. Yet she sounded flat, toneless. A hint of unhappiness, of desperation, came through in the tightness of her mouth, the darting eyes.

"I'm Gretchen."

"I'm Cindy," she said, offering her hand. "It's nice to see you again. I'm afraid I haven't met too many of the neighbors."

"You're renting from Mr. Rialto?"

"Actually, we're subleasing from the man who rented the house. He had to leave on business for a year."

"Oh," Gretchen said, relieved and sorry for Julia at the same time. "So you'll be leaving, then?"

The woman stepped out on the porch. In the brighter light Gretchen could see the sharp planes of her face, the hard edges. Her hipbones showed through her jeans like axes. Gretchen thought she must be about twenty-five, though she looked experienced, jaded.

"Yeah. Scott's out of work, anyway. We might go to Florida. Scott has family there. Maybe they can help him get a job."

"What does he do?"

"He's a carpenter."

The housing market was in a lull, she read every day in the paper. "My husband got laid off, too," she said, trying to be sympathetic.

"Me and Lorie," Cindy gazed affectionately at the little girl, "we'll just go where the wind takes us."

Cindy's nonchalance, bordering on irresponsibility, in Gretchen's view, shocked her. How could any woman be so cool when her future was a vast unknown? She thought of her own sleepless nights, the burning deep inside her stomach, the constant feeling that something terrible was about to happen.

"Do you want to go to Julia's house?" Cindy asked her daughter. Lorie nodded, her face transformed. "Okay. Be a good girl."

"I'll bring her home in a couple of hours," Gretchen promised. She noted Julia's radiant expression as well.

Gretchen led the children across the street and to the house. She was pleased that Julia would have a friend today, and even more heartened by Lorie.

As the little girl entered the house, she might have been stepping into a child's wonderland. She examined the toys in Julia's room as if they were priceless. Bucky and Julia watched her, as if surprised by her delight in toys they had gotten bored with long ago.

"Do you want to see my dolls?" Julia asked, pulling out a box from the closet.

Lorie curled her legs under her body on the carpet. "Are all those *your* dolls?" she asked, peering into the box. She waited.

"Go ahead! You can play with them."

Bucky squatted down, and Gretchen was pleased that Julia handed him a doll as well.

Satisfied that the children would be all right for a while, she closed the door halfway and found her mother in the living room. Carole had taken her shoes off, and lay on her back on the leather couch with her eyes closed.

Gretchen turned the radio on to the country station and curled into the easy chair, rocking.

"She seems like a lovely child," her mother said in a tired voice.

"I know. I'm surprised. With parents like that..."

"How old is she?"

"She says she's five. I guess she'll start kindergarten this fall, like Julia."

After a few moments Gretchen said, "I wish Julia had more friends over. The children entertain each other. It makes it easier for me."

"I know," her mother agreed. Then, "When is Rósa coming?"

"Tomorrow," Gretchen answered. "I can't wait. She really puts this house in order."

"She does," her mother agreed.

"How are you feeling, Mother?"

Carole shifted her weight on the couch. "Not too bad. That radiation makes my chest hurt, though. And I feel tired. I wish I could be more help to you. I wouldn't go through this, but the doctor thinks the treatments will give me a few more months."

You could, Gretchen thought, explain why you left Ted and me. But since her mother had arrived, and clearly felt ill, she had decided not to press her. She would be patient. She would bide her time and wait until her mother was ready to answer her questions.

At least, her smoking and drinking had decreased lately. Probably because she didn't feel well, Gretchen assumed. She thought of Ted, on assignment in the Philippines. Carole had not contacted him yet, wanting to wait until he returned to the United States in three months. Would he have a chance to see his mother again, alive?

"Sam's going to the bank tonight," Gretchen said.

"To find out about the loan? How wonderful!"

"His product's finished. He's been working with an engineer from the University. All we need now is the money."

"I admire Sam. He lost his job, but he made a whole new start. He sure is a go-getter."

"I know, Mother. But I'll feel a whole lot better once he gets back from the bank. It took longer than he thought to finish the business plan and apply for a loan."

"Of course, sugar." Carole sounded tired, distant. Leaving us again, Gretchen thought. In the last few weeks, in spite of herself, she had become fond of her mother. She had become accustomed to having her in the house. Gretchen had to remind herself to stay detached. Her mother was dying. There was no sense getting hurt all over again.

"Mommy, can we watch the Wizard of Oz?" The three children trailed into the room, Julia in front.

"Have you seen that movie, Lorie?" Gretchen asked.

"No." Lorie hid demurely behind Julia, her hands behind her back. From the couch, Carole turned her head and smiled at the child. Lorie had a cherubic quality–pearly-pink skin and rounded cheeks. With her shining hair and large, glowing dark eyes, she tugged at Gretchen's heart. The contrast between Lorie and her parents baffled her. How could a child remain unscathed, seemingly innocent, in the care of coarse people who drank and smoked and conducted loud parties until dawn? Lorie had the outward appearance and demeanor of Bo-peep.

"I'll turn the movie on for you, if you like," Gretchen said. Julia asked to watch it every day, and Gretchen continued to be concerned about her interest in Judy Garland's death. But she could hardly refuse now, when Lorie had never even seen the wonderful movie once.

When she came back from the study she picked up the newspaper. Her mother had dozed off. Gretchen's eyes roamed over the front page.

The Department of Water and Power had issued a warning to conserve water before ordering mandatory rationing, as Los Angeles entered a fourth drought year. The military services had asked Congress for permission to cut officers from the ranks, due to funding cutbacks. The Census Bureau was having trouble finding homeless people to count them, and President Bush refused to eat his broccoli. The country continued to fizzle as the recession took hold.

Gretchen closed the paper and lay back, suddenly overwhelmed by the turmoil of the world that seemed to invade her own life as well.

❄ ❄ ❄

When Gretchen and the children took Lorie home, the Bradleys, an older couple whose house sat kitty-corner from Lorie's house and next door to the anarchists, stood in their front yard watching her with obvious disapproval. For a moment, Gretchen questioned her motives. Maybe she shouldn't have anything to do with Lorie's family. But Lorie was not responsible for her parents, she thought, staring back defiantly. Today she had been a wonderful playmate for Julia.

"I hope she wasn't too much trouble! I'm Scott." The man approached from the house, wearing jeans without a shirt. A faded tattoo of a devil covered most of his chest.

Gretchen smiled nervously. "No! She was a pleasure."

Scott pushed Lorie under his arm with his big hand. Gretchen noted Lorie's trustful gaze.

Gretchen studied Scott. She saw a man with bad teeth and dark pouches under his eyes. A man who probably drank too much and slept erratic hours. A man who had lost his job, as Sam had, but who lived daily under his failure. A man probably bitter with the world, whom she would never trust.

"Lorie," Gretchen sank down to Lorie's height. "Can you tell your daddy about what we did?"

Scott laughed, his teeth filmed with yellow at the gum. "Oh, I'm not her daddy. I've just been livin' with them for a few months. Cindy and I rented this house together."

"I see," Gretchen said, her heart going out to Lorie. "Well, we played with toys and watched a movie."

Scott took Lorie's hand. "That's good. She don't have too many playmates. We appreciate you havin' her."

As he led Lorie into the house, Gretchen wondered what was worse: to have a mother under the worst of circumstances, or not to have a mother at all.

❄ ❄ ❄

At five-thirty, Gretchen heard Sam's car in the driveway. She rushed outside to meet him.

"How did it go?" she called.

He got out of the car slowly, gathering his briefcase, sunglasses and coat. He wore a shirt and tie–strange to her after three months of unemployment–and walked toward her, smiling.

"You got the loan!" she squealed.

"No," he said matter-of-factly. "I've been turned down."

She stopped short. "You got turned down?"

Sam shook his head. "Not enough collateral. Happens all the time. I thought the house would be enough, but since we took out that second–"

"Turned down," Gretchen repeated. She thought she would explode. Or simply die. She waited for her body to cave in on itself, rendering her a limp mess on the ground. What would be lost first–the cars, or the house? She imagined with horror having to explain to the first creditor that she couldn't pay.

"Don't worry, honey. I'll just have to go with plan B."

"Plan B?" she asked, trying to focus her attention.

"I knew there was a chance we'd be turned down by the bank. I'm going to do what most entrepreneurs do–ask my father for the money."

"Stephen," Gretchen said slowly, finding a crumb of hope. "Of course. Why didn't we consider asking him before?"

"I hoped we wouldn't have to. Maybe I was a little too confident."

"Maybe so," Gretchen said, exhausted, yet feeling her strength returning. "When are you going to ask him?"

"I'll call him tonight," Sam said, and together they went into the house.

❄ ❄ ❄

At dinner, Sam ate heartily of the baked chicken, steamed green beans and baked rolls Gretchen had prepared.

"...so, he'll send the money tomorrow, in a cashier's check. I need to look for an office, of course, and start pricing computer equipment."

The excitement at the table seemed infectious. The children picked at their food, mouths open, eyes darting between the adults. Carole sipped her wine, her cheeks robust, looking almost healthy. Gretchen played with her food, eagerly listening to Sam for details. She felt elated, and a little guilty over her prior tumble into despair. The money was on the way.

"I think it's so wonderful that your father can help you out," Carole said. "I wish I could..."

"It's okay, Mother," Gretchen said quickly. She and Sam knew her mother had only dwindling savings.

"He must be a very successful man," Carole said.

"Yes, he is," Sam said proudly. "He's a self-made businessman. He was in the army when he was young, and he used the G.I. Bill to go to electronics school. Then he built his own company. My mother worked to support us during those years when he was getting started."

"Really," her mother said. "Then he knows what you're going through."

"Oh, yes," Sam said. "And he thinks for me to start my own business is the best thing in the world. He was more than happy to help, once I asked him."

The best thing in the world, Gretchen heard. Why was this experience the worst thing in the world, to her? She would have to buck up, she resolved, change her attitude. If Sam's mother had had the courage to stand by his father while he got his business started, then she could do the same.

❆ ❆ ❆

Julia woke her sometime in the night. She stood at the foot of the bed, waif-like in her cotton nightgown. "Daddy," she whispered loudly. "I had *five* nightmares!"

Sam groaned and rolled to the side of the bed. Julia crawled in next to Gretchen and lay down on her back.

"Mommy," she said after a few minutes, when Gretchen was almost asleep again. "When I die I want to be buried next to you, and Dorothy, and the dinosaurs."

❆ ❆ ❆

The next few weeks passed in a frenzy of activity for Sam. He found an office, right on Ventura Boulevard, and began purchasing equipment. He hired a secretary to answer the phones and put an ad in the paper for support staff. Gretchen barely saw him, but didn't mind. She had a sense that things were finally happening, that the business had finally come together.

She spent most of the time with her mother. Carole needed more help now. Gretchen slipped into the role of caretaker with ease, a role she knew well. Cindy brought Lorie over to visit several times. The children played, leaving Gretchen time to spend with her mother.

One Friday, Gretchen accompanied her mother to see her doctor. Rósa stayed with the children.

"What time is it?" Gretchen asked. "How long have we been sitting here?"

Carole rubbed her temple. "It's three o'clock."

"We've been here for an hour!"

Carole shrugged. "This is a doctor's office."

"We had an appointment," Gretchen said. She walked over to the window. "How much longer until my mother can see the doctor?" she asked the woman at the desk.

The woman glanced at a rack of files. "Doctor's pretty busy today. You still have two ahead of you."

"We had a two o'clock appointment," Gretchen said stubbornly.

The woman regarded her as if she were an impertinent child. "I'm sorry."

"How many patients were scheduled for two o'clock?" Gretchen asked. The woman pursed her lips. Disgusted, Gretchen returned to her chair.

Finally, the nurse called Carole's name.

"How are we doing today?" she asked, as Carole stepped on the scale.

"Pissed," Gretchen said under her breath, but the nurse had already walked efficiently to the door of the office and placed Carole's chart in the plastic holder. Carole and Gretchen followed.

"Doctor will be a few minutes," the nurse said.

"How much longer does that mean?" Gretchen asked in irritation, slumping into a plastic chair next to her mother.

Twenty minutes later, Doctor Myers breezed cheerfully through the door. Without apology, he took a stool across from the women and opened Carole's chart. Gretchen sat up in rapt attention.

"Let's see, let's see. You finished your last week of radiation today? Yes. That's all you can have."

Gretchen and Carole waited. "We got the results back from your x-ray the other day. I must say, I'm surprised myself."

"Why's that?" Gretchen asked.

"The tumor has shrunk considerably."

Carole gripped Gretchen's hand.

"Now, as I told you, this cancer is incurable. But we've slowed it down a little. Now that you're through with your treatments, you should feel better for a few months. When it comes back, we can try more radiation, and possibly chemo."

Carole frowned. "My doctor in Texas told me chemo wouldn't be effective against my cancer."

Dr. Myers waved his hand dismissively and peered at her over his glasses. He reached over and touched Carole's knee. "Don't be such a pessimist. My philosophy is to try anything. Let's wait and see how you do for a while."

He'll put my mother through the mill to make an extra buck, Gretchen knew instantly. She noted her mother's hopeful face, Dr. Myers' condescending smile, and more anger and helplessness welled up inside of her than she had ever known.

When Gretchen and Carole rose to leave, Doctor Myers followed them to the door and patted Carole's shoulder. "You know," he chuckled. "I honestly never thought you would do this well."

"What a jerk," Gretchen said when they were in the car.

"What do you mean?"

"Mother! Can't you see how patronizing he was? He practically said you were hopeless."

Her mother was silent. Then she said in a small voice, "I thought he meant I had surprised him."

"He meant that he had given up on you from the start," Gretchen said with disgust. "He didn't expect much from you."

Carole stared out the window. Gretchen thought of the ravages of the disease yet to come. Future visits with this doctor. She wished that with a whisk of her hand, she could wipe out the cancer and the presence of Doctor Myers in their lives. Her mother hunched against the door, and suddenly seemed small and frail.

"I'll take care of you," Gretchen said, fiercely protective. Past emotions flickered, and a new, surprising strength. She sighed, gave her mother a reassuring touch, and started up the car.

Chapter Twelve

How did everything go?" Gretchen asked Rósa when she and Carole arrived home.

"Oh, fine! I took the children outside, for a walk."

The house had been picked up as well, Gretchen noticed, and the dishes in the kitchen sink washed. Gretchen had come to depend on Rósa. And now that Sam would be starting his business for sure, she wouldn't have to worry about letting her go.

"Have you...heard about your children lately?" she asked, wondering if Rósa would like to talk about them. Yet, she didn't want to cause pain by reminding her of her distant children.

"Look." Rósa's face shined as she reached into her old leather purse and withdrew a snapshot. "This came yesterday in the mail. These are my children."

Gretchen peered at the two children in the small color photo with brown overtones. The little boy was dressed in play soldier's clothing. The little girl, with her arm on her brother's knee, smiled with dignified seriousness at the photographer. She wore a simple blue dress with a box collar and short, straight sleeves, unadorned except for a thin strand of lace that edged the sleeves. With her hair cut bluntly short, she looked older than five and from a different era. Like a dark little flapper girl, incongruously caught by the camera as she squatted next to a tiny soldier.

"They're adorable," Gretchen said finally. "The little girl, she looks just like you. Does your son look like his father?"

"I think so," Rósa frowned, examining the boy's face. "It's been so long since I saw Javier."

"Oh," Gretchen continued cautiously. "Then he did live with you?" She thought of what Sam had said about women being raped, left alone to raise the children.

"Oh sure, until after Sandra was born. We weren't married, but we were, how do you say...common-law?"

"Is he...fighting in the war?"

"Yes. Javier, I haven't seen him for three years. Maybe he is dead, I don't know."

Gretchen's heart ached for Rósa. "You must be so proud of him, though. He's fighting in the army, if he's still alive. He's fighting for his country."

Rósa seemed confused. "He doesn't fight with the army. He fights with the guerrillas. Against the army."

"*Against* the army?" Gretchen asked in surprise, suddenly seeing Rósa in a new light.

Rósa nodded.

"Oh," Gretchen said, embarrassed. "I thought...I thought he was fighting for his country."

"He is," Rósa said emphatically. "He went to fight with the guerrillas after the army soldiers burned our town and kidnapped our young men. The Cristiani government and the army, they do not represent our country. They represent the wealthy people who own land."

"Really?" Gretchen said, dismayed. "But how..."

"You see, a very few rich people own most of the land in El Salvador. The pesanos...peasants who work the land, want better conditions. They want to own land, and farms. The wealthy people don't want to give up control. They send the army to punish us when we ask for better wages and conditions. For schools and medicine."

"I see," Gretchen said, horrified. "Do you wonder about him much?"

"To do so is very sad for me. So many men have been lost, and killed in this terrible war. I don't have too much...hope."

"But...isn't the United States giving money to El Salvador? Surely, that must help you."

"The United States gives money to the army, not the people of El Salvador! The money is used to buy guns and bombs that kill our people."

Gretchen had never seen Rósa so upset. "But why...?"

Rósa shrugged. "Your president sees communism everywhere. Even if our guerrillas received arms from the Soviet Union, communism is not the issue. Human rights is the issue."

She stared again at the children in the photograph.

She could see now that the children stood beside a mound of dirt, and wore no shoes. A windowless house with chipping paint made up the background of the picture. The poverty seemed to reach out and cloud the children in the picture, giving them a yellowish, dull cast. Gretchen had an image of heat, and flies and dust and disease that threatened to close in on the perimeter of the photograph, merciless and unceasing.

She handed the picture back to Rósa, trying to contain her sorrow for her children, and her own guilt. Wasn't she somehow responsible? That she had gained, and Rósa suffered? Perhaps Sam's company had made some of the bombs that had ended up in El Salvador. Her prosperity, Rósa's loss. Suddenly, she felt ill.

She considered her own life, rich and privileged, that stuck out like a glittery show piece. Her trips to the health club while Rósa cared for her children. The racks of her clothes that seemed ostentatious compared to the three simple dresses that Rósa owned. And when she romped with her children in the backyard, laughing at Bucky's wide-armed attempt to catch a ball, she was disturbingly aware of Rósa. Rósa, kneeling on the cold bathroom floor, scrubbing to make the porcelain tub as white as she possibly could.

❄ ❄ ❄

One morning two months later, Gretchen raced down the hall after Bucky, who darted into Julia's room, giggling. "Come back here, you little stinky pie!" she called.

Julia was at school, but would be none too pleased to have Bucky in her room. Gretchen grabbed him by the shirt, swept him into her arms, and carried him to his own room.

"We're going to Daddy's new office today," Gretchen said as she changed him on the floor. "And I want you to look nice."

Her mother stood at the doorway. She wore a lime-green, cotton pantsuit that made the bags under her eyes more pronounced, her skin more pale. Her hair, once as red and curly as Gretchen's, had faded and stuck up in tufts. She no longer wore her makeup, and appeared older. She coughed spasmodically, and Gretchen gave her a worried glance.

"I guess I should go in for an x-ray," her mother said. "My last blood panel looked so good, I've been...hopeful that I might feel well for a while."

"I know, Mother," Gretchen said, her heart going out to Carole. Doctor Myers had warned them that the remission wouldn't last for more than a few months. Now the worsening symptoms, her mother's hacking cough and increasing weakness, struck Gretchen with dread. She knew her mother had been happy these last few months in the Carey household. As the time with her mother dwindled, she raged inside at times, railed against the unfairness of her life and her complete helplessness against her mother's illness.

"I'll call the doctor for you when I get back," Gretchen said, stifling her grief, trying to be upbeat for her mother's sake. "I'm taking Bucky to Sam's office. I'm anxious to meet this new office manager."

"I hope he can get things rolling," her mother said.

"Well, the office has only been open for two months. We can't expect great sales right away. Still, we've got to start advertising more. Sam says this manager is a marketing whiz."

I don't want my mother to know how worried I really am, Gretchen thought. I know she wonders at times if she's a burden. I shouldn't have expected a miracle when the office opened. Sure, Sam's made a few sales of his product to car dealers. Still, after the bills, he's barely bringing in enough for groceries. We've only got enough to pay the mortgage for another three months. After that...

"Sam has a good sense about business," her mother said brightly, and Gretchen hoped she was right. Sam remained ever-confident, but she had to wonder. True, he had put together his office efficiently. He had hired two programmers, a secretary, and a college student to ship out the product.

Gretchen pulled Bucky into a blue, short-sleeved shirt and a striped red coverall. She finished tying his shoes and said, "I think I'll take him out for a hamburger after we visit Sam. Rósa should be coming soon to start on the windows."

Before Carole could answer, there was a knock on the door. Gretchen peered out the peephole and saw Cindy on the porch. She opened the door.

"Lorie wanted to play with Julia today," Cindy said in her nervous, smoker's voice, almost jittery.

Bucky came up behind Gretchen's knees and stared at Lorie. The little girl's face broke into a dimpled smile.

"Julia's at school today. I'm sorry, Lorie."

Cindy seemed agitated. "Actually, Gretchen, I have to go to work. Scott didn't come home last night. My sister's out. I don't know what to do with Lorie."

Gretchen pressed her lips together. This was the second time Cindy had asked her to baby-sit Lorie. She didn't want to become involved in Cindy's problems. And she didn't want to be considered a ready baby-sitter for Lorie.

"I don't mind watching her," Carole spoke up. "How long will you be gone?"

Cindy's expression turned hopeful. "Only about three hours. "And Lorie's so easy. She won't give you any trouble, I promise."

From the last incident, Gretchen knew it would be more like five hours. But Lorie was an extremely easy, pleasant child to have in the house. At least compared to Julia, who tended to mope and whine, or Bucky, who had become more demanding and insisted she pick him up or play with him all the time.

"Are you sure you're up to it?" Gretchen asked her mother protectively.

Carole gave her a reassuring wave of her hand. "Of course. Lorie's a jewel. Don't worry about me."

"All right," Gretchen said, a little reluctantly. "But I'm taking Bucky with me. I guess she can watch a video or something."

"Goody," Lorie said pertly, and stepped into the house.

"Thanks, Gretchen," Cindy said. "I really appreciate this."

"All right. But maybe you ought to find a baby-sitter."

Cindy bit her lip. "Well, usually Scott's home. But he hasn't been able to find a job, and...he's been drinking a lot more lately."

"I'm sorry," Gretchen said lamely. After Cindy left she wondered if she had made a mistake in letting Lorie and Julia become friends. Sam thought Cindy and Scott were "bad news", with their Saturday night parties that continued to disturb the neighborhood and the constant presence of Scott's unkempt motorcycle friends. But Julia and Lorie played so well together...maybe there wouldn't be any more problems.

She strapped Bucky into his car seat in the passenger side of the Volvo and pulled out of the driveway. Bucky reached his hand over to touch her hair as she drove, and when she looked at him he gave her one of his smiles that was pure gold.

She'd hate to say she had a favorite, but Bucky was still in the angelic stage, and so cuddly and heart wrenching. She supposed that when he was talking more and a little older, he would be just like Julia, argumentative and sullen. But for now she enjoyed him, and her time at home with him.

Sam, an only child, had panicked when she had gotten pregnant again. He had feared the additional demands and disorder another child would mean in their lives. Whether she would have a boy or a girl had not even seemed a factor in his concerns.

Then she had spotted slightly in the fifth month, and the doctor had ordered an ultrasound. Sam had stood by her side as the doctor moved the device around on her stomach, the three of them watching the vague figure that was the baby on the monitor.

"I can't tell what anything is," Gretchen had said in frustration. "It looks like this blob that just keeps wiggling around."

Sam, staring intently, had suddenly lunged in front of the doctor, pointed at the screen and yelled: "It's a, it's a... PENIS!!"

Gretchen, squinting at the monitor, waited anxiously for the doctor's confirmation. He had laughed and congratulated Sam on his son. After that, Gretchen had been surprised at the change in Sam's attitude, but nonetheless pleased.

She drove down Ventura Boulevard until she came to the building, a row of storefront offices facing the street. She pulled into the driveway and parked in the back.

When she walked in the back door, carrying Bucky, she was astonished to see a large aquarium in the lobby. Brilliantly colored fish, in yellow, blue and red hues, swam about in the crystal water.

"My goodness, what's this?" she asked Jackie, the new secretary, who sat behind her desk opening mail.

"Like it?"

Gretchen turned her head to see a tall, sandy-haired man grinning at her.

"I'm Dave, the new office manager," he said, offering his hand.

She put down Bucky, who immediately ran to stare at the fish. "I'm Gretchen Carey. And yes, they're beautiful. I just never expected..."

"The boss's wife. I think any successful company should have an aquarium in the office," he said. "Don't you agree?" He smiled at her a little flirtatiously.

"Of course," Gretchen said and smiled right back, although he didn't interest her in the least. She was accustomed to the response she invoked in men, especially when she wore tight jeans and cowboy boots, like today. She knew that when men saw her, and heard her accent, many thought she was dumb and sexy. She didn't mind, really. When she was underestimated, it gave her an advantage.

"This is your aquarium?" she asked. "What kind of fish are these?"

"Salt water, the only kind," Dave said. "I have two more tanks at home."

"My goodness. Did you bring this one from home?"

"Uh-huh. I moved it in a few days ago on my truck. Don't you think it adds a touch of class to the office?"

"Yes," Gretchen admitted. Bucky continued to watch the fish, as if transfixed. She moved closer and stared through the acrylic.

"What's that?" she asked, pointing at a creature on top of a large piece of coral.

"That?" He moved closer to her, his shoulder brushing hers. Deftly, she moved away, giving herself room. "That's an anemone. See the little clown fish inside its tentacles? He has a symbiotic relationship with the anemone. The tentacles are poisonous, but a clown fish can live safely inside, even share the animal's food. That's a sea urchin there." He pointed to a round, spiny creature. "And that's a turbo snail."

"Turbo snail?" Gretchen laughed.

"It eats the excess algae like a little vacuum cleaner. It zooms around the tank at night and helps keep it clean."

She watched the aquarium with fascination. The stunning fish darted through cavernous holes in the coral. The tentacles of the anemone waved delicately in the water.

"I feel like I could stand here and watch this for an hour," she remarked. "I guess I can see why you like aquariums."

He moved closer, and she let him. Sizing him up, she decided he was harmless. He would get no encouragement from her. Even if she weren't married, he wasn't her type. She had little interest in men who were too forward. Who came on obviously, thinking they were smooth, as if she would be flattered by their attention.

Ignoring Dave, she remained captured by the colors and rhythms inside the tank. The peaceful beauty.

"It's remarkable, isn't it?" he asked.

"Yes."

"What do you think the appeal is?"

"What?" She thought the question rhetorical.

"You know. We're waging a war against nature. We're mowing down the forests, driving thousands of species to extinction, poisoning the sky and the seas."

She glanced at him sharply, ill at ease. He had described the source of her greatest concern.

She swallowed. "Yeah?" she said, wondering what he was getting at.

"Man is becoming more and more alienated from the natural world. You know that. But right here," he said, touching the top of the tank, "you have an exquisite slice of nature. That's why I love aquariums. When I look at these fish and animals I can be in touch, even if artificially, with the beauty of the natural world. I feel that connection that we all long for. That we've lost."

"Why not just get a puppy?" she said cruelly, suddenly wanting to distance herself from him. He moved away from her, to her satisfaction, and looked at her as if he thought she had understood nothing.

But his words struck a deep chord in her. She had been lonely in Los Angeles. Not just for friends–Terry was one of the best friends she had ever had–but for the wide open spaces in Oklahoma. She missed the clear skies, the Indian summers, the hard autumn rains. The mistletoe that grew rampant on the black oak trees across the state. Lake Eufaula, where she had frequently swum with her father and brother. And the Arbuckle Mountains, where she had escaped the city on camping trips.

She had hated Los Angeles at first, especially when she and Sam lived in the apartment. Now that they lived in a quiet, wooded neighborhood, she didn't mind so much. But she still hated going into the city, or to malls, or on the freeway. She worried about the destruction of the planet with an increasing awareness. The loss of the natural world that Dave had described.

"It really is gorgeous," she said finally, trying to be nicer. "Is it hard to take care of?"

"I have to change some of the water once a month and clean the filters. Other than that, it's just a matter of keeping algae off the sides."

"What about that salt on top?"

"Ah, yes." He opened the cabinet under the tank and took out a rag. "The salt accumulates every day, which is kind of a pain." Carefully, he wiped the rag over the hood.

Bucky had lost interest in the fish and was pulling open the drawers in Jackie's desk. Jackie, an older woman who looked like she might have grandchildren, smiled at Gretchen knowingly.

"Where is Sam?" Gretchen asked her.

"He's at the dentist."

"Oh," Gretchen said, her spirits falling. "I didn't know he was going."

"A filling came out this morning," Jackie said.

"That figures. Come on, Bucky, let's go get something to eat. It was nice to meet you, Dave. Your aquarium is gorgeous."

"I'm glad you like it," Dave said. "Sam wasn't so sure about the idea, but now he agrees it makes the office. His product is going to be hot, by the way. Once we get some ads in a few big auto magazines and get sales rolling, this place is going to be hopping."

"Really?" Gretchen asked excitedly.

"I promise. We're so sure about it, we just doubled the equipment."

"Huh," Gretchen said thoughtfully, a little disturbed. "Sam didn't mention that to me. Well, I'm glad to hear you're so confident. That makes my day."

Chapter Thirteen

❦❦❦

After lunch, Gretchen took Bucky to do some errands and shopping. When she arrived home, close to three o'clock, she found Rósa sitting at the dining room table, crying.

"What is it?" Gretchen asked, rushing to her side. Carole sat beside Rósa, her face grim and tear-stained as well. Lorie peeked out from Bucky's room, then disappeared inside again.

"My...my children. My children have been...," her voice rose in a wail, "killed!" She broke down, sobbing into a hanky, her shoulders shaking.

"My God!" Gretchen cried. "Oh, no. No, I can't believe it."

When Rósa calmed down she said, between hoarse sobs, "The bombs fell last night. One went through the ceiling of my sister's house, into my children's room. My son was killed instantly. My sister took my daughter to the hospital, but she...died on the way. Ay Diós," she broke down again. "My babies."

"And she showed up for work today," Carole said grimly. "She was afraid of losing her job."

Gretchen pulled a chair next to Rósa, put her arm around her shoulders, and let her sob. "Do you want to go home?" she asked quietly.

"The apartment," she rasped. "It is so empty. The memories..."

"You stay here. As much as you want. You can sleep in the other spare bedroom, if you want to."

How could she do or say anything that would ease Rósa's heartache? Rósa had already suffered so many losses. The pain of women...how could anyone who didn't have children understand what it meant to lose a child? Such pain must be...unendurable.

She stayed with Rósa for a long time, holding her while she sobbed uncontrollably. She grieved for the two children she would never meet, who had lost their lives so senselessly. She railed against the torment of war. Who was responsible for such an atrocity? Who could she blame?

When Sam came home that evening, Bucky and Julia rushed to the door to meet him. "Daddy, Daddy!" Julia cried. "I made you a picture at school!"

"I made you picture!" Bucky echoed, though he hadn't.

"Hi, honey," Sam said tiredly, setting down his briefcase in the corner. "I'm sorry I missed you this morning. I suppose Jackie told you about my tooth–Dr. Mosier wants to put a crown on it, and did the prep today."

"I see," Gretchen said, her voice flat.

"Hi, Carole!" Sam said, loosening his tie as he walked into the living room. "Did you have a good day?"

Carole glanced at Gretchen. "Pretty good. I was with Lorie this morning."

"Oh, that's good."

"Lorie was here?" Julia asked in a disappointed tone.

"Her mom asked us to watch her," Gretchen told her. "You can play with her tomorrow. Sam, I want to talk to you about something."

"I'll go make the salad," Carole said. Gretchen already had a meat loaf and potatoes baking in the oven, and the warm smell of browning meat wafted through the house.

Gretchen sat on the couch and Sam joined her. He waited. "It's about Rósa. Her children were killed in a bombing last night."

Sam's eyes instantly darted to the children, who stopped arguing over a sample box of cereal from the mail and stared at their parents.

"They're going to have to know, Sam."

"I suppose," Sam said, looking upset. "My God, that's terrible."

"I know."

"How...how is she?"

"Devastated. She couldn't stop crying. I took her home a little while ago."

"Doesn't she have somebody? A sister, or something?"

"She lives with her cousin."

"God, what can you say to her?"

"I don't know. There was nothing I could say that could possibly help. But her cousin said there's a support group for Central American refugees in Sherman Oaks that meets the day after tomorrow. I told Rósa I would take her. Maybe that will help her. I don't know. If they were my kids," she shuddered, "I don't know if anything or anybody could help me."

"I'm amazed she's even ambulatory," Sam said glumly.

"Yeah."

"Mommy." Julia came over to Gretchen, her expression a mixture of childish curiosity and apprehension. "What happened to Rósa's children?"

Gretchen drew Julia to her. "They were killed, sugar."

"Is she sad?"

"Yes, she's very sad," she said, straightening Julia's curls on her forehead.

"Did their skin fall off?" Julia asked blithely.

"Jesus Christ!" Sam said angrily.

"It's all right, Sam. She doesn't realize...no, Julia. It takes a long time for that to happen."

"Are they going to be buried in the tar pits?"

Sam listened, his expression irritated.

"No, sugar. Rósa's children lived far away, in another country. I'm sure they'll be buried there."

"Are they in heaven?"

"Yes," Gretchen said miserably, as her eyes filled with tears. "I suppose they are."

❄ ❄ ❄

Gretchen picked up Rósa two days later and drove her to Sherman Oaks. The meeting was in a church. Outside, a sign on the wall said, "Survivors of Central American Wars."

Gretchen had come to the realization that nothing she said or did would take away any of Rósa's pain. All she could do was be there for her, and listen.

As they walked up the steps to the door, a man came out of the church and approached them. "My name is Luís," he said. "Are you here for the meeting?"

"Rósa is," Gretchen said. "I'm her friend, Gretchen."

Rósa and Luís exchanged words in Spanish. Rósa cried constantly since her children died, and clutched a wadded handkerchief in her hands.

Gretchen stood by with Bucky in her arms. Her eyes kept drifting to Luís. He was only a little taller than she was, but solid. His white cotton shirt, open at the throat, strained against well-developed arms and shoulders. With his impeccable posture and proud bearing, he appeared larger. The smooth planes of his face were tight, with high cheekbones under olive skin. Clean-shaven except for a well-trimmed mustache, his black hair was free of any gray. He appeared to be in his mid-thirties. Gretchen glanced at his left hand, but didn't see a wedding ring.

Luís touched Rósa's shoulder. He turned intense, cinnamon-brown eyes on Gretchen. "I will take care of her," he said. "Are you coming back for her? In an hour-and-a-half?"

Gretchen nodded. "Yes," she promised. "Of course I will." She felt flustered, nervous. She was unaccustomed to a man other than her husband having an effect on her.

She took Bucky to a nearby park and the time went quickly. When she returned to the church, she found Rósa inside. Several people stood around her, and she seemed deep in an emotional conversation. Gretchen hesitated in the aisle, not wanting to intrude.

Luís stepped over to her. He's too handsome, she thought, trying not to stare at his face. I feel like an idiot...surely he can tell I'm attracted to him. Then guiltily, she remembered Rósa. Self-consciously, she waited for him to talk, feeling transparent. She searched for Bucky. He sat on a bench, kicking his feet, listening to the talking group.

"She's had a terrible shock," Luís said.

"How is she? Do you think the support group helped her?"

"Oh, yes. I think it helped her to be with people from her own country. These people have had similar losses. They understand."

"I'm glad." She lowered her eyes. "I didn't know if...anything would help her."

Luís was silent for a moment. Then he said, "You are a very good friend. She speaks highly of you."

"We...we're very fond of Rósa. I wanted to help. If my kids..."

"Yes. She has suffered a very great tragedy."

"Are you involved in this group?" she asked stupidly.

"Yes, of course! I started this group."

"Then, you're from El Salvador?"

"Yes, but my family came to the United States fifteen years ago, before the war. I still have aunts and uncles and cousins in El Salvador, though. I am very active in the FMLN, the resistance movement against the Cristiani government in El Salvador. I try to help the many refugees who come to this country, who have lost loved ones. Besides this group we have a referral network for jobs, immigration and housing."

"That's wonderful," Gretchen said. "Rosa has told me a lot about El Salvador, and the war. What...what kind of work do you do?"

"I am a lawyer. Most of my work is in helping the refugees."

"I see." This is a man of convictions, she thought. No wonder I find him...appealing. What if Sam found a purpose to believe in, and work that really mattered? That's what Sam is missing. I never realized it before now. For years, Sam made bombs, simply for the money. Now he's chasing another money maker. There's nothing wrong with a computer program to enhance car brakes, but still...why doesn't Sam feel the same concern, the same sense of responsibility, for the problems in the world?

Something shifted inside of her. Something small, but nonetheless powerful. She suddenly realized why she felt drawn to Luís. With him she shared the empathy for Rósa's pain, the pain of all suffering people. Which Sam found simply depressing.

"Will I see you next week?" Luís asked, his gaze direct, and she knew then that he was equally attracted to her.

I shouldn't see him again, she thought. This feels...dangerous. Yet, I do want to help Rósa. "I'll bring Rósa," she told him.

She saw his face brighten, ever so slightly. "I will see you then, Gretchen."

❆ ❆ ❆

When Gretchen arrived home after dropping off Rósa at her apartment, the first sound she heard was Carole's coughing.

"You don't sound very good at all," Gretchen said when she found her mother lying on her bed.

Carole coughed again, deeply. She put a hanky to her mouth, and Gretchen saw the stain of blood.

"Come on, I'm taking you to see Dr. Myers."

She helped Carole into the car. The kids piled into the back seat. After Dr. Myers was able to see Carole, he talked to Gretchen in the hall while Carole got dressed.

"I've given her some medicine to help her cough and stop the bleeding. But this chest x-ray shows that the tumor has grown, and in fact, two others have shown up as well."

Gretchen's spirits sank. "She was doing so much better after the radiation."

"Radiation will knock a tumor down for a while. But I told her when I took over her case that she didn't have much time."

Gretchen winced at his choice of words. "What can we expect next, Doctor?"

"She'll keep getting weaker. The cancer will probably start to spread. I'd like to put her in the hospital, where I can monitor her and try some other treatments. Do you still insist on keeping her at home?"

The image of her mother in a hospital, being subjected to uncomfortable tests and procedures until the very end, turned Gretchen's stomach. "Yes, of course. We want her at home."

"All right, then. That's your decision, but it won't be easy. Let me know if you change your mind. Have a good day."

Gretchen walked after him. "Wait a minute! What do we do next? What about her pain?"

Dr. Myers assessed her with slightly reddened eyes, the kind of eyes that all doctors seemed to possess from years of not enough sleep. "We can give her more radiation. We can do that on an outpatient basis."

"I don't think she wants to go through that again," Gretchen balked.

"Okay, that's up to you."

"But what about her pain?" she repeated.

"Mrs. Carey, this is it. Your mother is dying. I'll give her a stronger medication. We'll see how that works."

He took a chart from the back of a door, entered the room, and closed the door. You son-of-a-bitch, Gretchen thought. This is my mother! This is my life! She glared at the closed door, incensed at his callousness. She hated her helplessness, hated the prospect of her mother's pain and terrible death, hated the responsibility that she didn't know if she could shoulder.

If only Sam...but Sam was immersed in his business now. Half the time, he came home for dinner then went back to the office until late. They had barely spoken about anything important lately, except briefly when Rósa's children were killed. She felt an ever-widening distance from him that alarmed her. Yet, she didn't know how to stop it. She should be happy that his business was up and running, that Dave had so much confidence in it. Instead she felt strangely displaced, apathetic and despondent. Her life off-kilter.

The faces of her mother, Rósa and Terry entered her mind. And then Luís, emerging in the background. As she left the building with her children, her arm around her mother, a sensation like a loud clanging rang through her head, pounding, giving her no peace for the rest of the day.

Chapter Fourteen

Mother?" Gretchen came into the dark bedroom, reluctant to disturb Carole, yet wanting to tell her the news. The July heat pervaded the house, even at ten in the morning; Gretchen would turn on the cooler soon. She knew the heat bothered Carole, and made her even more uncomfortable and lethargic.

Carole coughed and sat up. Gretchen helped her adjust the pile of pillows at the headboard. "Guess what? Ted is coming!"

"Ted! Oh, my stars! I can't believe it. This is wonderful. When?"

"In two weeks." She had called her brother, who had returned from the Philippines to Colorado, and told him he had better come. Their mother might have another month or two, but not much more.

"Ted. A master sergeant in the Air Force. I am so proud of my kids. I'll tell you." Another spasm of coughing racked through her. "I am so happy."

Thank God, Gretchen thought. Her mother had become depressed lately, and had aged and deteriorated. Gretchen hoped a visit from her brother might help Carole enjoy what life she had left, and perhaps die in peace.

Ted had not been anxious to come; she had pressed him. He barely remembered his mother at all, and felt no connection to the dying woman whom Gretchen and Sam had taken in. But she herself had certainly benefited from these few last months with her mother. If she felt unresolved, even bitter at times about her mother's abandonment, she held out hope that Carole might still reveal why she left her family.

Gretchen went to the kitchen to get her mother some juice and her morning medications. She had dressed in a long, pale blue cotton skirt and a sleeveless blue blouse. Her favorite kind of outfit in summer.

"I already squeezed her some juice," Rósa smiled. Since her children had died, Rósa had come to the house almost every day. Gretchen hadn't been able to pay her much, but Rósa seemed to find comfort in taking care of Carole and the children. Now that Sam's business was taking off, and she expected to have some money again soon, she would give Rósa a raise.

"I don't know what I would do without you," Gretchen said. "She's needing so much care now. If you weren't here–I couldn't afford to hire a nurse."

"No, we will take care of Mrs. Simpson. You do the right thing, Señora, to take care of her at home."

"You're a gem," Gretchen said, and reached over to kiss her on the cheek. How a woman who had lost so much still had so much to give, she would never understand.

"I'm having lunch with my friend Terry today," Gretchen said. "Can you give Mrs. Simpson her pills at twelve? Then I'll drive you to your meeting when I come back."

"Of course, I will," Rósa said. "Later, I will help her with her bath as well."

❄ ❄ ❄

She met Terry at a children's hamburger restaurant with a new play area that included a tall slide that ended in a ball pit, climbing structures and a small merry-go-round. The children ran screaming to play. Gretchen and Terry sat at a table watching the kids, waiting to order lunch.

"You look nice today," Terry remarked.

"Thanks," Gretchen smiled. "It's wonderful being able to buy new clothes again."

"It must be. You guys were living on the edge for a while, weren't you?"

"Well, we never went broke. But I don't know what we would have done if Sam's business hadn't picked up the way it has."

"I think that's great!" Terry said. "In less than a year, Sam has changed occupations and made a whole new start. You told me he was ambitious, but I think this kind of success is pretty damned admirable."

"Yeah, I guess it is," Gretchen said. "I don't know...this past year has been kind of like being...lost."

"What do you mean?"

"I mean that it's easy enough to get excited about things *now*. But for a long time, every day, I didn't know if there was really any hope. Sam didn't have any doubts, but that's just the way he is. Wondering about whether you're going to lose everything does something to you after a while. It makes you angry inside, and wears on your self-pride. Sometimes I would take Julia to school and go to the health club, and wonder if I really belonged. If I had any right to be there anymore. I resented these lawyer and doctor's wives, in their fancy cars. People who don't know what it means to worry about a home for your children, and decent food and clothes. I felt guilty, like an impostor. Like I was shedding my skin and turning into something ugly. Does that make any sense?"

"Absolutely!" Terry said emphatically. She shifted in her seat, the gold bracelets on her wrist jangling. "God, talk about stress. To lose one's livelihood, especially with a family. If that wouldn't erode your self-esteem, then I don't know what would. And you didn't even have any power to do anything about it! Sam was holding all the cards. No wonder you felt helpless and angry."

Gretchen squirmed. How did Terry manage to uncover her most secret feelings? Especially her resentment toward Sam, which now seemed mutinous, considering his success. "But...he took care of us. He started his new business."

Terry shrugged. "I know. But everything hinged on whether he could make that choice work. And while you waited and worried, all you had was your faith in him."

"I have a lot of faith in Sam," Gretchen said. She could barely acknowledge to herself, let alone Terry, her current disillusionment with Sam.

"How's lover boy?" Terry asked with a mischievous gleam in her eye, and Gretchen thought the timing of the question strange.

Gretchen knew she referred to Luís. Maybe she should never have mentioned her feelings for him. Sometimes, she thought her friend seemed to egg her on, pushing her into thinking about things she would never think about on her own.

"I'm just attracted to him, that's all! I see him every week when I take Rósa to her meeting. But all we talk about is Rósa, or the weather. Nothing is going on, and nothing ever will."

"Hmm. Okay." She sounded unconvinced.

Gretchen felt irked, but had no plausible comeback. She watched Terry leap up from the table and run to Holly. The little girl stubbornly tried to climb up the slide, to the annoyed protests of the children at the top of the ladder.

"Get in line and wait your turn," Terry said firmly to her daughter.

"So what's this about your brother?" she asked when she returned to the table.

Gretchen leaned back in the plastic chair and put her hands in her lap. "Well, he's coming next weekend. Gosh, that's going to be a scene. Ted barely remembers my mother. Now he's going to meet her before she dies."

"That's good, don't you think?"

"I don't know," Gretchen said thoughtfully. "As much as I've grown fond of her, I wonder if it would have been better if she'd never written to me. If she hadn't come back."

"Why?" Terry asked.

"I have to go through her death again," Gretchen said softly. "That's how it felt as a child. Like she had...died."

"I'll bet it did," Terry said soberly. Then they were quiet for a few moments, watching the children.

"How about if I order lunch?" Terry asked, breaking the mood.

After they had eaten and the children returned to play, Gretchen asked, "What about that man at work you were interested in?"

Terry gave her a puzzled look. "Oh, you mean Carl?"

"I think so."

"He hung up on me."

"What do you mean?"

Terry shrugged. "I mean, I liked him. I thought he was interested, if I can trust my intuition. I tried to talk to him about it, and he backed off and acted like a stranger. He put me in my place."

"Why?" Gretchen stirred her soda with her straw.

"Who knows?" Terry said broodingly. "Fear of commitment, fear of me knowing him. Fear of knowing me. Fear of getting close. Fear. Who the fuck knows. He hung up on me."

"I'm sorry. What did you do?"

"I ignore him now," she said maliciously. "He doesn't even get it, but I don't care."

Gretchen listened, the single world seeming like an alien, hostile place.

"My first lover was an older man, when I was twenty-two," Terry said. She stared off past the play equipment, to the street beyond rippling with cars. "He was so sweet, and caring. He loved me in a completely nondemanding way. It seemed so easy, and natural. You know," suddenly her gaze turned piercing, straight into Gretchen's eyes, and for an instant Gretchen felt like Terry was seeing inside of her. "I believe a relationship with that first lover is so powerful, so intense, that most people spend the rest of their lives trying to find that same relationship over again."

Gretchen stared at Terry blankly.

"What's the matter?"

"What you...you said," Gretchen stammered. "About a first lover. That just reminded me of...someone...someone I used to know." And she was flooded with memories of Andy, and ached for him as if she had been with him yesterday.

She had been sixteen when she met him. She had taken a job in a horse stable three afternoons a week, where she cleaned stalls and exercised the horses. Andy had been a trainer, thirty years old. He had been tanned, with eyes like chips of sky. Inside the faded jeans and plaid shirts he wore, he moved like one of the animals he tamed.

He had been kind to her, and let her exercise a gentle stallion whose owner had become ill. She had been shy at that age, and had grown up leery and cautious of the airmen on base. But she had warmed to his laughter and the calm way he handled the horses. After a few months she looked forward to going to work so she could be with him.

One day, as she helped him scrub leather bridles in the tack room, he had drawn her to him, his arms on her waist as if she belonged to him. He had kissed her like she had never been kissed, deeply, and she had broken away from him and fled in panic and confusion.

Two days later, when he touched her again she didn't pull away. She had never felt so wanted, and could not remember arms holding her like that. So strong, and warm and safe. He made love to her in his trailer two weeks later.

She had been with him for a year. Her father never knew, and to her knowledge, no one at the stable knew, either. They had been discreet, especially because of her age. But one day, another girl told her that Andy had kissed her. Devastated, Gretchen quit her job, and saw him only a few times after that in town.

She had cried over him for two years. What had she been thinking of? She was too young. He wouldn't have married her. But sometimes, when he had moved toward her in a dark stall and she had pressed her cheek to his chest, his flannel shirt soft and smelling of horses, she forgot the dreariness and mediocrity of her life. She felt special, ecstatically in love, her hunger for him taking over her consciousness. When she came with him she saw bright light beneath her eyelids. Stars, she had called it. And to this day, she had never again felt the same passion, and longing, and the total sexual bliss that she had known with Andy.

❄ ❄ ❄

Later in the afternoon, when Gretchen went to pick up Rósa after the meeting, she waited outside the church for Luís. She sat on a shaded stone bench while Bucky headed over to the small play area. Every week, Luís came out to talk to her while Rósa finished inside, a routine Gretchen had come to look forward to. Surely there was no harm, she rationalized. She found Luís interesting and enjoyed his company.

"Gretchen! How are you today?" He came up from behind her and found a place a short distance away from her on the bench.

"I'm fine, I guess. How is Rósa?" Although she saw Rósa almost every day, she never pressed her to reveal her feelings and moods. At the support meetings, she knew, Rósa confided her anguish over her lost children to the men and women from her country who understood and who had suffered similar losses.

Luís reached for a twig on the ground and spun it between his fingers. He looked up to watch Bucky, who was making endless trips down the slide. He moves with such easy confidence, Gretchen thought, so at home in his body. She thought of Sam, so tense and easily irritated.

"I think she is doing okay," Luís said. "The worst shock and grief have passed. Still, she thinks of those children every minute of the day, and dreams about them in her sleep. Some weeks, she says she has nothing to live for. It's very...hard for her. I think the only thing that helps her is taking care of your mother. She feels needed."

"I'm glad," Gretchen said quietly. "I can't think of anything worse than for a mother to lose her children. I don't know how she'll ever fully recover." Then startled, she thought about her own mother. Although Carole had left, her children had been lost to her for so many years. Had Carole grieved the same way Rósa did? Now that she knew her mother better, somehow that seemed possible. The insight filled her with pity for Carole. Who had helped her mother, in her grief?

"She is lucky to have you," Luís said. "You are a very good person, Gretchen." When his eyes sought hers, she felt his gaze almost melting into her. She warmed under his stare, soft and pliant. Then he reached over and stroked her cheek with the backs of his fingers. An experimental touch, as if he waited for what she would do.

She pulled away from him like a fugitive on the run. Standing abruptly, she mumbled something about Bucky and ran over and snatched her son from the slide. "I'd better see if Rósa's ready to go," she said, avoiding his eyes. I can't see him again, she thought. He can never touch me again and I will forget about him. This is nothing. It doesn't matter. Now that Sam's business is succeeding, everything will be perfect again. I don't need this man.

As she walked out with Rósa she saw Luís standing outside, talking with two women. He turned toward her, his expression hurt and pondering. She smiled mechanically and gave him a short wave, then turned her back and walked stoically to her car with Rósa.

"Is Luís...married?" she asked Rósa on the way home.

Rósa gave her a knowing glance that made her feel exposed. "I hear he is divorced recently. He has one son, who I think is fifteen."

"Oh. He is a very...interesting man."

"Yes. A very good man. Do you think your mother would like to sit outside on the porch later when it gets cooler?"

Again, Gretchen realized that as her mother grew more ill, Rósa's grief over her children seemed to diminish. She had a new purpose in life. Someone to nurture, someone who truly needed her. And strangely, although she would never wish her mother to be dying, she felt grateful. She was powerless to help her mother, and Rósa had become immersed in her care. Something good would come out of her mother's illness.

Rósa remained quiet for the rest of the trip home, her face toward her window. She seemed to be thinking of things, feeling things, that Gretchen could not imagine. When she tried, the horror of the images in her mind sent her reeling back to the way she had felt when Luís had touched her face.

❄ ❄ ❄

A week later, on a warm morning with a blue sky that sparkled with light, Cindy asked Gretchen to watch Lorie while she went to work. She promised that Scott would pick her up after two hours.

"I don't really mind," Gretchen told Carole. "She's a pleasure, and Julia enjoys playing with her so much."

Her mother was up, sitting in the easy chair in the living room. A blanket covered her lap, despite the heat. She seemed to have her good days and her bad days. The last few days she had felt better, her cough quieter.

"When is Ted coming, sugar?"

"Soon," Gretchen said patiently. Her mother had become more forgetful lately. Gretchen knew it was due to the narcotics Carole took for pain. Still, she felt like she was losing her mother, bit by bit.

"Can you get me the pictures?"

"Of course." Gretchen brought a photo album in from the den containing pictures of her and Ted growing up. Her mother had become consumed with looking at the pictures every day, asking questions, as if trying to fill in the years she had lost.

"Señora," Rósa said, coming in from the kitchen. "Can I bring you some lunch now?"

Carole grimaced. "I'm not hungry."

"How about some nice fruit salad?" Rósa pressed.

"Hi!" Sam's voice came from down the hall, and the door slammed.

"Sam! What are you doing home?" Gretchen asked, surprised to see him in the middle of the day.

"Hi, ladies," he said as he set down his briefcase and plopped down on the couch. "We just filled another big order and got it into the mail this morning. Dave runs that office like a pro...I couldn't have found a better manager. So, it's such a beautiful day, I decided to come home for lunch."

He smiled brightly at the women: Carole, on the easy chair with the picture album open on her lap; Rósa, standing nearby in her old, pink seersucker dress. And Gretchen, by her mother's side. The women stared at Sam, and suddenly, to Gretchen, his presence among them seemed so strange and intrusive. Of all the people in the room, Gretchen felt she knew Sam the least. The realization troubled her.

"Daddy!" Julia came out of her room and ran to her father, followed by Lorie and Bucky.

"Who's this?" Sam asked cheerfully, motioning to Lorie.

"This is Lorie, Julia's friend!" Gretchen said, amazed that he didn't know. "Lorie's here almost every day."

"Well, not when I've been here," Sam said, and Gretchen wondered how much else he had missed. Her own life kept barreling along, a daily drama with her mother, and Rósa and the children. But her life with Sam had drifted off course. It's not his fault, she thought quickly, biting her lip, guilty at the criticism she felt. I owe everything to Sam. Now that the business is stable, we've got to catch up. Before we get any further apart.

"I guess I'll go make a sandwich," he said, rising to his feet. She didn't know if he was truly hungry, or if he needed to escape the watchful gazes of the women in the room. Gazes that regarded him not as a welcome member of the family, but as a stranger who had little to do with their own, real lives.

Chapter Fifteen

❦❦❦

Lorie! Scott is here," Gretchen called, after peering through the peephole in the door. It was four o'clock, and Lorie had been here for more than four hours. She felt a little annoyed that he hadn't come for her earlier, as Cindy had promised.

"I'she ready to go," Scott slurred, swaying on the porch.

Gretchen regarded him with disgust. What a pig, she thought, with his dirty, unshaven face. His bleary eyes and stinking breath.

He was clearly drunk. "Where is Cindy?" Gretchen asked, hesitating to send Lorie home with him.

"She'll...be home in a few minutes," he said. "C'mon, Lorie, le's go."

Lorie joined him on the porch. Her own children crowded behind her silently, watching Scott. Lorie's face assumed that numb, guarded expression that Gretchen had seen her take on lately with Scott. He held her hand and led her down the driveway.

It breaks my heart to let her leave with him, Gretchen thought. The son-of-a-bitch! If only I could do more to protect Lorie.

The next afternoon, as Gretchen began preparations for Ted's visit, she heard a knock on the door and found Lorie standing on the porch.

"Honey, where's your mom?" Lorie had never come over by herself. Her mother or Scott always walked her across the street.

"Can you please call the police?" Lorie said, as if she were asking for a popsicle.

"What?"

"My mommy wants you to call the police. Scott is hitting her."

"Come in here, Lorie," Gretchen said quickly, taking the child by her arm.

Gretchen took her into Bucky's room, where Bucky was playing with cars. Carole was sleeping in her room. "Stay here," she said firmly. "I'll be right back."

She ran across the street and over to Lorie's house. Before she could start down the dirt driveway, she heard Scott's angry voice, then Cindy's cries. Something smashed and broke inside the house.

She returned home and called the police. She waited on the living room couch, watching the street through the window. Lorie came into the room holding one of Julia's dolls.

"Did you call the police?" she asked.

"Yes, I did." She drew Lorie beside her on the couch. "Are you okay?"

She gave Gretchen one of her angelic smiles and nodded.

"Has Scott hit your mom before, honey?"

She walked the doll along the arm of the couch. "Sometimes," she said. "Sometimes he gets mad at her and hits her." Gretchen noticed that her voice sounded like a baby's.

"Does he ever hit you?"

"No," she said, and went back to play with Bucky.

Gretchen saw two police cars pull over outside Lorie's house. She went outside to the street and watched. Four officers disappeared into Lorie's house.

Mrs. Doheny came out of her house in her bathrobe and rubber gloves. She stood watching the police cars. A few cars passed by, and then Gretchen saw two officers leading Scott, handcuffed, out of the house. Compliantly, Scott slid into the back of a police car. Both police cars drove away, and Mrs. Doheny returned to her house, muttering and shaking her head. Gretchen went inside.

"Come with me, Lorie. I want to talk to your mom," she said. She hoisted Bucky onto her hip, and took Lorie by the hand.

"Cindy," she called through the torn screen door. "It's Gretchen!"

Cindy opened the door. She had obviously been crying. Her face appeared mottled. A purple bruise covered part of her cheek, which had begun to swell. Beneath her eyes, her mascara had smudged and caked.

"Come in," Cindy sniffled.

Gretchen entered the dark house and followed Cindy to a set of faded green couches. The house seemed neat and in order except for a small table and a lamp, toppled on the far side of the room. Then she saw the kitchen, and the broken glass strewn all over the floor.

She wondered why Cindy didn't open the drapes–heavy, monstrous green drapes with a tasseled fringe and two huge tasseled cords at each end. But Cindy seemed to prefer the darkness. She curled up on one end of the love seat, her feet bare.

"Scott's just been getting meaner and meaner since he lost his job," she said in a husky voice, lighting a cigarette. "And he's been drinking so much. I don't know what to do."

"Can't you...leave?" Gretchen asked, her first reaction. Bucky sat in her lap, examining her keys, and Lorie had joined her mother on the couch.

"Where would I go?" Cindy asked, futility in her voice. "Scott and I have problems, but I don't want to be alone. I don't think I could make it by myself."

"Wouldn't it be better to be alone, than to be beaten up? What is this doing to Lorie?" Gretchen said, then immediately regretted the judgmental sound of her questions.

Cindy wiped away tears from the corner of her eye with her little finger. Her eyes looked bleary. Although Cindy was only in her early twenties, at that moment she appeared old, haggard.

"I know. I try to take care of her but still...it's hard. I keep hoping Scott will straighten up...if only he could find a job! We're going to be moving on soon, anyway. We got an eviction notice from Mr. Rialto last month. We can't pay the rent."

"Where will you go?"

"Florida. Scott's brother might be able to get him a job down there."

Gretchen felt torn as she listened; her own husband had lost his job. She vacillated in her desire to help Cindy and Scott, and especially Lorie, and the need to detach herself from these people who brought her own fear of poverty so painfully into focus.

How close had her own life been to slipping into the same fate as Cindy's? She didn't know. Sam's new business seemed to be succeeding. What if it had flopped? What if it went under? And Sam, in his failure, turned abusive? Leaving her adrift with two children. Even in the compassion she felt for Cindy, her situation was too close, too threatening. The raw images of the worst scenario that had tormented her for months now.

"I hope he'll get a job, Cindy. I'm sure he will," Gretchen said, then gathered Bucky to leave. "I have a friend," she said impulsively, thinking of Terry. "She might know something...like a counseling group for you and Scott. Something like that. I could call her, and ask."

"Okay," Cindy said, and Gretchen caught the interest, the need for help.

She left, and a tremendous feeling of relief washed over her as she entered her own home. She walked across the polished foyer and into the living room, with the clean white walls that practically glittered. She tread across the spotless ivory carpets, and opened the white French doors that lead into the shady patio in back.

For a frightening moment she saw her home, her very place in life, as an illusion. She saw a fragile, temporary structure that could disappear into dust despite her most vocal claims to it. Her home, that reflected the life she believed she was entitled to and had entrenched herself in, suddenly appeared transitory and etherial.

She imagined herself in Cindy's home, battered in the darkness, feet bare, listless on the couch. She felt horrified that she could even see herself that way. Cindy and Scott were too close, the walls of her own home too thin. She wished she could distance herself, extract them from her neighborhood and her life and her thoughts. Suddenly exhausted, she set Bucky down and pulled off her boots, only then realizing that Cindy had not even remembered to thank her.

❄ ❄ ❄

"If that guy comes back here again, I think you should call the police," Sam said when he got home. Gretchen had gone to bed, but had turned on the light and propped some pillows under her back to talk to him. She had related the story of how she had called the police on Scott earlier in the day.

"I will," Gretchen said. "I hope that doesn't happen. I just...feel so sorry for Lorie and Cindy."

"Hopefully, they'll move soon. I won't miss those people, that's for sure."

"I'll miss Lorie," Gretchen said with a pang.

"Julia can find a new friend," he said, climbing into bed with her.

"Lorie is a special little girl. I really love her."

"Yeah, but that *family*...! Hey," he said, a gleam in his eye. "I bought some champagne. I thought we might celebrate now that the business is taking off. How about it?"

"Sure," she said, feigning enthusiasm. Of course they should celebrate–his achievement had surpassed her best expectations. They were out of danger now, the rough time had passed. Yet, why didn't she feel happy?

Sam brought in the bottle and two glasses. "Here's to us," he said, and she joined him in a toast. Us. The word carried a different meaning than it once had. Once, he had adored her, and she had looked up to him. They had been tight and solid in their lifestyle and rising, lucrative prosperity. She had known her place, and her place had been with him.

Now, she wondered about her recent disenchantment with him. He had become immersed in his business, that was all. His only purpose was to support his family. An inarguable, noble cause. She felt grateful, relieved, now that the business had succeeded. Of course she did. The distance came from within her, she realized with astonishment. Sam smiled at her, and as she gazed at his familiar face a sadness overcame her that she strived to conceal.

She had changed. The death of Rósa's children had left her aware in a troubling way of the inequities around her. She now thought of the years Sam had built weapons, and their own financial success, and felt empty, shamed, an accomplice to the destruction of Rósa's life and others like her. When she saw herself in Cindy's eyes she saw a woman who had become privileged and complacent, selfish in her material needs.

Sam seemed to have no idea of her conflicts and thoughts–she was still his wife, the same old Gretchen, who supported him and deferred to him in loyalty and marital habit.

He put down his glass, turned to her and possessively cupped her breast. She slid toward him. Her confusion mounted as he began to stroke her slowly. My husband, who has taken care of me and my children, she thought, trying to place her feelings. She closed her eyes, drifting. But as he made love to her, a part of her stubbornly held back, dulling her responses. The secret, hidden part of her that guiltily, involuntarily, longingly and ecstatically, yearned to be with Luís.

❄ ❄ ❄

Sometime in the early morning, the ringing phone woke them. For a moment, Gretchen thought it was the alarm, and hated the thought of getting up. Not yet, she thought. She rolled over and brought her knees up close to her chest, clutching the covers around her chin. The ringing persisted, then stopped.

"What?" She heard Sam's voice, nasal from sleep. "I don't believe it! Oh, God!"

Instantly, Gretchen sat up. Sam hung up the phone. He lay back, both hands covering his eyes.

"What is it?" she asked, fear spreading inside her.

"There was a fire. That damned aquarium. I should never have let Dave set it up in the office. Salt corroded a wire from the heater, apparently, and started an electrical fire. All the computers, the software. Everything is gone."

She had never heard him cry. She had never heard the deep moaning, choking sounds that came from him. From some deep place she hadn't known existed. He turned his back to her. She didn't dare touch him. Not yet.

Is this what it's like to be paralyzed? she wondered. Her entire body felt numb, as if she had been pushed off a cliff, and lay with a million fractures. She was maimed, with no hope of recovery.

She didn't know how she could feel so calm. Her mind felt paralyzed, too. She thought of tomorrow, the future, but her mind was dark. She could see the past in vivid colors, though, and suddenly clung to her memories tenaciously. Then the tears came, though still calmly.

She remembered Dave's exquisite aquarium, like a stolen jewel from nature. Its inhabitants sequestered from the wildest depths of the oceans, to dwell amidst the huge urban sprawl of Los Angeles. Out of place and probably unwilling in their artificial block of synthetic sea water. Dave's attempt to connect with the diminishing natural world that had ironically, unexpectedly, caused the destruction of Sam's new business. She pictured the aquarium, probably toppled and melted, and the dead sea creatures that lay in the ashes of Sam's business. What a shame, she thought. What a shame.

Chapter Sixteen

Two weeks after the fire, Gretchen and Sam waited silently at the round table in Mr. Greenway's office while he checked the figures on Sam's policy.

Mr. Greenway shoved a form toward Sam. With a pencil in his hand, he pointed to the figures.

"What?" Sam almost shouted. "Forty thousand dollars? Those computers were worth eighty!"

"Yes," Mr. Greenway said patiently. "But you only insured forty thousand dollars worth of equipment."

Gretchen clenched her fingers together. "Sam," she said in a small voice. "After you got the second set of computers, did you change the policy?"

Sam's face turned ashen. "I thought...I thought Dave would do that." Desperately, as if unable to accept the lost money, he demanded, "How did you arrive at these figures?"

"Well, we have a computer model..."

"What kind of computer model?" Sam glared at him.

"A model called fuzzy logic. That's how we determine what we pay out. We start with a value–"

"I know all about fuzzy logic!" Sam said hysterically. Gretchen stared at her lap, horror-stricken.

"Come on, Gretchen. Let's go," Sam ordered, rising and stumbling out the door.

"Your check will be in the mail..." Mr. Greenway called after them.

"What is he going to do now?" Carole asked Gretchen a week

later, as if afraid that Sam might hear. She asked that question as if she were spinning in the same nameless void as Sam, a place empty of answers and solutions. The women could hear Sam playing piano in the living room. He had been playing all morning.

"His job interview is tomorrow," Gretchen said, trying to sound more assured than she felt. The warm morning sun streamed through the bay window in the kitchen, where the women were finishing a cup of coffee.

Gretchen had been endlessly counting the hours as she waited for this job interview, as if it were a life raft in a nightmarish storm; a slim, yet tangible possibility for hope that had become a gigantic obsession as the days passed with crushing slowness.

She found herself picturing the company, the men who would decide if Sam would have this job, and sent them silent pleas. Thinking positively and imagining success can be very powerful, she had read once in a self-help book. For the past week she had concentrated so hard on Sam landing this job that her neck and shoulders had become tense and sore with her effort.

At times, she prayed to God, even if God's role in her life had become increasingly unclear. Where a short time ago she had felt blessed, she now felt abandoned to this obscure and degrading situation that made her wonder why. Why is this happening to us? When we were set for life, with only better things to come.

Her mother slurped her coffee and set down her cup. She still insisted on getting dressed every day, and wore cool, pink cotton sheeting shorts and a white blouse. Her medicines controlled her cough and pain. Except for moving stiffly and needing more rest, she remained fairly lucid most of the time.

"Do you think he's all right?" her mother asked. "Since the business burned down he's been so...moody."

"No, Mother. He's not all right. I don't blame him. But I don't know what to do..." She felt on the brink of tears, as she had every day since the "incident". Nothing had been left–the equipment, Sam's product, their hopes and dreams. Her worst fears had been realized–they were on the verge of being broke, with no quick plan to save them.

Then she had gotten the bill from her mother's insurance company. She didn't want her mother to know. The insurance was indeed good, but covered only eighty percent of Carole's treatments. Currently, the bill totaled fifteen thousand dollars. Enough to break them.

"Did he call his father last night?"

Gretchen slowly shook her head. "Stephen. He's furious. He called Sam an idiot, and a complete failure."

"Oh, no!"

Gretchen nodded grimly. "The eighty thousand dollars he lent us is down the drain. He wants us to send him whatever we get from the insurance company. He said Sam is going to have to bail himself out of this one, and stand on his own two feet."

"I'm sorry, sugar," Carole said. "How can a father be so hard on his son?"

"Stephen is a success nut. He made it on his own, and he holds Sam responsible for the fire. He thinks Sam was...careless."

Gretchen went into the living room and listened for a few minutes as Sam continued to play.

"I didn't see you," Sam said gruffly. His appearance shocked her: his hair dirty and uncombed, and his shirt wrinkled and carelessly buttoned. He hadn't shaved since the fire.

"Sam, I think you're going to get that job tomorrow," she said, trying to sound convincing.

"What makes you think that?"

She fumbled for words, frightened by his anger. Lately, he had treated her as if he couldn't stand her, as if she were even the cause of all their current problems. "Because...because you're a brilliant engineer. I know you'll get a job."

He banged his fingers on the keys, making a horrible sound. He glared at her with puffy, reddened eyes. "What the hell do you know about anything? About the real world?" He continued to stare at her, and she stepped back, reeling from the brunt of his hostility. "You have no education. No concept of real life. You didn't even know your mother's insurance company wouldn't cover the whole fucking bill!" He turned his eyes away, fingering the chipped ivory piano keys. "You've been getting a soft ride for the last six years."

She felt the color drain from her face. She trembled, not from fear, but from hurt.

"I've been out *there*–" he pointed savagely, "while you've been doing the health spa, the park, your papier-maché animals. Giving our money away to your goddamned Blind People and Elephant People and Pet People and who the hell knows what else People! And I don't know what to do!" He buried his head in his hands, his shoulders shaking. "I just...don't know what to do."

She moved toward him, cautiously touching his shoulders. When he didn't pull away, she slid beside him on the bench and put her arms around him, laying her head against his back.

Sam remained motionless, his head bent in defeat. When the business had burned down, she had felt hope disappear, and the return of the same gnawing terror she had experienced after Sam's layoff. But her fears and disappointments paled, compared to his rejection.

"Sam," she said softly. "Don't you love me anymore?"

"Oh, honey." He swiveled on the bench and held her tightly in his arms. "I didn't mean it."

"Sam...don't you think this is a time for us to face together, instead of bickering?"

"I just...feel so depressed about the business. We had it made, Gretchen. It would have been a big success, I know it. I don't mean to hurt you." He sighed, dropping his arms. "But it's hard for me to be very affectionate right now. I think we need...to sort of face this on our own. At least I do. I don't have the energy right now for a relationship, to give you what you need."

I need you, she screamed inside. Don't abandon me now. But she drew away, knowing that any demands she made would be construed as another pressure on him.

Dejected, she went out to the backyard to see her children. At least she still had Julia and Bucky, who loved her unconditionally. And when she gathered them in her protective arms, she could momentarily overcome her fear and loneliness. The haunting feeling that the people she loved were slipping away.

Later, as she and Sam rested in their bedroom while the children napped, Gretchen said, "Sam–we've got to talk about the money."

"It's all gone!" He covered his face with his hands. "All because I got so caught up, I didn't increase the insurance policy. How could I have been so stupid?"

How indeed, Gretchen wondered suddenly. She had trusted Sam. He had reassured her so many times that he knew what he was doing, that he would take care of everything and she needn't worry. All she knew was that if she had been in charge of the business, that fire insurance would have been adequately increased.

"Is the mortgage paid for this month?" she asked.

"No!" He waved his hands, almost frantically. "We can pay it, but we won't have much left for the rest of the month. I put everything into that business. And now that I've mailed Dad back his money...if only we didn't have your mother's bill."

"It's not her fault. She understood everything was completely covered."

"Maybe so! But you have to admit, that bill is going to drain what we have left."

She thought for a moment about family obligations. About love and fate and responsibility. She didn't blame her mother. Regardless of the burden her mother had placed on Sam and herself, she didn't regret her coming back.

"How could Stephen do this to us?"

"He doesn't understand how times have changed," Sam said, as if he had given the matter some thought. "He doesn't realize that there are limited opportunities now. He still thinks that if you have a dream, and work hard enough, you can succeed."

"I see," she said dismally. "Look. I'll cancel the health club. I'm putting Julia in public school when she starts kindergarten. And of course, I'll have to let Rósa go."

He offered no protest, only lay back in silence.

"What are we going to do?" she asked. The question had plagued her in her nightmares over the last few months as she waited for Sam's business to start. When she would wake up sweating and gasping for breath in the night. She had staved off the terrifying question while her faith had lain with Sam's business, hoping she would never have to ask it. Now their lives seemed reduced to a basic, core question of survival. What were they going to do?

"We have to put the house on the market. Just in case I don't find a job in time. If I don't get this job tomorrow, then I'll keep on looking. And in the meantime, I'll apply for unemployment insurance."

Her house. No. She couldn't lose her home, the only home her children knew. For him to suggest selling it felt so final, so definite.

She knew that to blame him, to be bitter, was useless. He had been irresponsible. But how could any of them have known that the aquarium would set fire to the office and burn it down? To see him so humbled hurt her and left her even more shaken. Clearly, he was coming apart. Even though he had not been responsible for the fire, he blamed himself for the plight of his family. He carried his guilt every day in the stoop of his shoulders, his inability to look her in the eye, and his withdrawal from the family. If she did blame him at times, felt exasperated with him, she was even more concerned about him. And she had no idea how to help him.

Chapter Seventeen

❦❦❦

The following Saturday, Gretchen drove by herself to the airport to pick up Ted. Waiting in a chair near his gate for him to disembark from his plane, she closed her eyes and wondered what she would tell him. That Sam interviewed for two jobs, but didn't get any offers? That he sleeps and plays the piano all day? That soon, our savings will be gone and we'll be living on unemployment? She thought about the last time she had seen Ted, over Christmas. She and Sam had been flying high. Ted, settled into his career in the Air Force, had admired their lifestyle and success. Now, their lives had taken a fall. Suddenly, she felt her pride tumbling as she envied her brother his security, the predictability of his life. His steady income with regular promotions.

"Gretch!"

Startled, she opened her eyes as he bent over her, and then she was in his arms.

"How are things going?" he asked as he picked up his luggage and they started for the exit.

"Rough," she admitted.

"I'm sorry," he said. "I thought you had it made."

She laughed cynically. "Do you remember when Dad was supporting Grandma in that nursing home, and we didn't have money at times for milk or bread, and we ate canned stew for days until Dad got paid? Things aren't that bad yet, but...I'm afraid."

"I wish I could help," he said.

"I know. But you, and Dad...you can't imagine what our expenses are out here, with the house, and the cars, and the bills we have." The responsibilities hovered over her like dead weight.

"Are you nervous about seeing...her?" Gretchen asked him on the way home from the airport.

He glanced out his window. "Naw. I don't know her."

"But, don't you...?"

"She ran out on us, Gretch." He cut her off, his voice hard and angry. His gaze turned straight ahead, and suddenly his profile seemed like a statue, still and hard and devoid of emotional life. She stared at him, fascinated. Growing up, they had rarely discussed their mother. In collusion with their father, she and Ted had eventually come to ignore Carole's absence, and eventually the hurt and loss and anger.

"Ted...I know you're angry. But she's sick."

He shook his head in amazement. "What about us? You want to let her hide behind her disease. But what about us?"

She had somehow assumed Ted would be amicable, forgiving now that Carole was dying. That he would be at least as forgiving as she herself was. But he didn't know his mother at all, she reflected. He only knew her as a memory, a woman who had abandoned him without reason. He hadn't had any time, as she had, to know their mother. He hadn't seen Carole's vulnerabilities, her pain. He hadn't had the chance to grow protective of her.

"Why did you come?" Gretchen asked quietly.

He turned his face toward her, surprise registering on his features. "You asked me to!"

"I see," she said in disappointment, dreading the impending reunion.

After a brief silence they talked about their father, and his new passion for gardening. She was pleased to hear Ted's voice, with the same, slow inflections as her own. As a child, and then even as a teenager, he had been compliant and easy. He had trusted her to make decisions, buy his clothes and drive him to friend's houses or the mall.

She looked at him, then turned the car onto Ventura Boulevard. His hair had been trimmed to regulation Air Force, with white-walls around the ears. His skin was lighter than her own, more freckled. He liked wearing his dog tags around his neck, even though it wasn't required. He had pulled them out from his shirt and, holding both sides of the chain, twirled the tags like blades of a tiny fan.

Her brother had grown into a man who didn't smile easily, who despite being sweet, lacked in insight and imagination. The Air Force suited him, she thought. He spent his free time watching sports on television with his buddies, a beer in one hand, the fingers of his other hand drumming on any available surface.

"How did you like the Philippines?" she asked.

"I liked it all right."

"What about that girlfriend you had there?"

"Oh." He brushed something off the legs of his pants. "Tam, you mean?"

"I guess. Do you miss her?" She glanced over at him.

"Yeah, sometimes."

"You didn't want to marry her?"

He grinned, as if at a joke. "No, Gretch. I wouldn't have married her."

She knew then that he had used this Filipino girl for sex, and to clean his house, and felt disgust for him.

"How long can you stay?" she asked, pulling into her street.

"Four days. That's all the leave I have right now. And I don't see the point–"

"It's okay," she said quickly, unable to bear any more of his rejection of their mother. "Things are kind of...tense right now."

"I'm sorry. Do you think Sam will find a job?"

"I hope so. But there's just not a lot out there right now, especially for someone in nuclear weapons technology."

"Bummer," he said. "Defense is getting cut a lot. What this country needs is another good war."

"Do you really believe that?"

He shrugged. "Our economy is based on defense. Wars have always boosted the economy."

She didn't know if he was right. But even if a war would boost her and Sam back into prosperity, she would not wish it. Somehow, the world had to change, and men had to change. Sam must be able to earn a living without the potential deaths of thousands of people on his hands. Something had gone askew. Why else was she now in this situation?

❁ ❁ ❁

They walked into the house. Carole rose from the easy chair as they entered the living room.

"My son. My baby," she cried, walking stiffly toward him.

She put her thin arms around him, her face joyful. Ted shuffled uncomfortably, and after a few moments disengaged himself from her embrace.

"You don't remember me at all, do you honey?" their mother asked. Ted's body seemed to visibly coil, to tense up, and he put up his hands in a gesture for distance. He still wore his dark glasses.

The pain in the room seemed so apparent, so brittle, that Gretchen had an overwhelming urge to jump between Carole and Ted. If only she could quiet this anger, this utter rage that she had seen building since picking him up at the airport. The worst thing was Carole's obliviousness, as she stood overjoyed and vulnerable, on the bare precipice of realizing her son's complete rejection. Did her drugs and her euphoria at seeing Ted after so many years give her a buffer, like anesthesia?

Yet, Gretchen stood apart, unable to interfere. Carole continued to smile, regarding her son with joy, unaware of the boiling rage that filled the room. A rage, she realized, that had surfaced during the first year of their mother's absence. She had shared in that rage, she knew it like she knew her love for her children, and her brother had every right to it. As that emotion pulsated from Ted with the raw power of an electrical current, she stood back and watched like an observer, transfixed. In the distance she heard the sounds of the television, the high voices of Sam and the children.

"I...*do* remember you!" Ted said, his hands at his sides now, his body shaking with tension. He gulped in air, agitated, and Carole's smile disappeared from her face. "Damn it. I remember you. And I want to know why! You coming here, and not telling us, is *shit*. It's gone on long enough."

He pointed his finger at Carole, his face crumpled, and he covered it with his hands. Gretchen bit her lip hard, tears blurring her vision. Carole looked into Gretchen's face as if stunned, and Gretchen stared straight back with no apology, no sympathy. Ted was entitled, and he had said what she hadn't had the nerve to say.

Carole reached toward Ted, then withdrew her arm. She blinked as if confused, and Gretchen feared that Ted had pushed her too far.

"I have so much shame," Carole said suddenly, in her broken, twangy voice. "Shame can almost kill a person. Did you know that?"

She seemed about to fall, and Gretchen helped her into the easy chair. She glanced at Ted. He moved to the couch and waited with his arms on his knees, fingers touching. His face softened a little with expectation. He appeared exhausted, and for the first time in years he resembled the little boy he had once been.

"Your father is a good man. But we never should have gotten married. It was a mistake, except for you kids. My mother raised me alone, after my father died. She taught me to strive for a better life.

"Your father was going to school when we met, through an extension program at Edwards Air Force Base. He was an airman, but he planned to finish school and apply for Officer Training School. After we married, he got transferred. Then he got transferred again. He gave up on finishing school. I hated being the wife of an enlisted man. Oh, not because of snobbery. But because we were second-class in the Air Force, and had so little money. It was a hard life for me.

"In Okinawa, I started drinking. I became an alcoholic, and needed help. But your father turned away from me. He blamed me for not having any self-control. He got colder and colder.

"By the time we got to Oklahoma, your dad and I were so far apart." Carole had started to cry, and Gretchen handed her a tissue from a box on the coffee table. "I was so ashamed of my drinking, but I didn't know how to stop. Then I met Phil."

Phil? Gretchen stared at Ted in astonishment, but his expression remained unchanged, his eyes on his mother.

"I met him in a restaurant in Del City, where I stopped one afternoon for a drink. I kept going back to meet him there. He was a businessman in Oklahoma City. He drank, too. But I had been so lonely, for so long. He was nice to me and rarely asked questions about my family. Well, I got pregnant."

Gretchen sat bolt upright. Never, in all the years she had wondered about her mother, had she ever surmised there was another man. Nor had she suspected a pregnancy! Did she have another brother, then? Or a sister? Why had her father never revealed any of this to her and Ted?

Carole coughed deeply, and Gretchen brought her a glass of water. "I didn't know what to do," she continued finally. "I started getting sick, and your father figured it out. We hadn't slept together in a couple of years, so he knew it wasn't his. Well, he went into a rage! He called me a whore. He made me pack and leave. Believe me, there was no way I was going to leave you kids. I went to a motel and called Phil. We talked, and he said he didn't like kids. And how did he even know it was his? He walked out, leaving me there on the bed in that hotel room."

Her mother's face took on a green color, almost ghoulish. Her hair stuck up in the back, and the circles under her eyes appeared like bruises. Gretchen could barely imagine her mother so long ago. Young, and caught in the throes of two men.

"I tried to go home," her mother continued. Her chin began to quiver. "Your father pushed me off the doorstep, then dragged me to my car and shoved me inside. He told me never to come back, that I was an unfit wife and mother. I drove back to the hotel, sobbing."

Gretchen clenched her jaw at her father's cruelty, her mother's pain. She determined to listen, and not to cry.

"I called my friend Jenny in Texas, and told her I was in trouble. We had gone to high school together before her family moved. She asked me to come stay with her until I got things straightened out. I ended up staying until the baby was born, and then for three more years. When I tried to call, your father hung up on me. I wrote to you, but I'm sure he threw away my letters."

Gretchen reached for a tissue and wiped the tears that appeared despite her attempt at control. She had been lied to by her father. She had never known how her mother had suffered.

"I was so sick with that pregnancy." Her mother's voice grew faint. "Then the baby was born, a little girl. I named her Megan.

She was underweight at birth. When she was four weeks old, she died. It was sudden infant death syndrome, crib death." Carole sobbed, and began to rock gently in the chair, as if in excruciating pain.

"I know why she died." Her voice was a wail, piercing Gretchen to her spine. Then she spoke so softly that Gretchen moved beside her mother's chair, taking her hand. "She died because I drank so much when I was carrying her. I murdered my baby." She broke down and sobbed, fresh tears squeezing from her eyes with each raspy breath.

Gretchen held her mother's hand tightly, and glanced at her brother. Ted remained motionless on the couch, his gaze full of judgments, of condemnations.

"Mother," Gretchen said hoarsely. "I never knew."

"Do you see how much I hated myself?" Carole demanded. "I had a nervous breakdown after Megan died. I was so depressed for so long. I did manage to get my drinking under control though, most of the time. When I recovered enough, I got a job in a department store. Jenny was wonderful–she had just been through a divorce, so she was happy to have a roommate. She tried to get me to go to Alcoholics Anonymous, or try therapy. I never went...I should have. But at the time I didn't think I deserved to be happy."

Carole reached down tentatively to stroke Gretchen's hair. Her fingers were wet with her own tears, and her daughter's. "I am so sorry. You kids are the ones who suffered. I lost my children, but after so many years, it's amazing what can be endured. You lost your childhoods. Over the years I became more and more convinced that you would hate me if I came back, if you knew the truth about the terrible things I had done. Then last year when I got sick...I had to take a chance that you might want to see me."

Gretchen gaze returned to Ted. Emotions shifted over his face, and then she saw him look up at his mother. A searing grief passed over his features, and tears welled in his eyes.

"Can you ever forgive me?" Carole asked, sobbing.

"It's all right, Mother," Gretchen said. She knelt and put her arms around her, then Ted was beside them, his arms encompassing them both. "It's all right."

❄ ❄ ❄

Several weeks after her visit with Ted, Gretchen called Terry. "Terry? This is Gretchen." She held the phone to her ear with her shoulder as she reached into a kitchen cupboard for Julia's coloring books.

"Gretchen? Is something wrong?"

"I just...don't feel very well," Gretchen said, her voice breaking.

"Can you come over?" Terry said instantly. "We could talk."

When Gretchen arrived at Terry's house, she marched into the bright front room with gold wallpaper and yellow slanted blinds over the windows. She sank into Terry's plush blue couch and set her foot up on the glass coffee table. Overdue for a haircut, she had pinned the hair off her forehead with one of Julia's barrettes, purple and shaped like a butterfly. Her green eyes, red-rimmed and tired, fixed on a bouquet of carnations and baby's breath on the coffee table. She gathered her thoughts.

"I don't even know what to say. I don't know what's wrong with me. I just feel like–I can't get out of bed in the morning. I can't go on anymore. All I want to do is cry."

Terry settled into a wicker chair on the other side of the table. She pushed her hair over her ears, her expression compassionate. "Oh, Gretchen. I see you suffering, and I wish I knew what to tell you. I wish I had a magic cure."

"I don't know what to do," Gretchen said, her voice almost a squeal. "What can I do? I think about that day and night. I can't sleep, I'm so worried. We don't even have enough money to pay the car insurance this month. I have to use credit. Sam...he's gone on job interviews, but hasn't gotten any offers. And it's not his fault! Companies are laying off, not hiring. He spends most of his time sleeping, or playing his piano. I feel helpless. I don't know what's going to happen to us."

"Have you thought about looking for a job?"

"I don't see how. I don't have any skills that would pay much. I can't leave my mother now, and the kids need me. Even if I found a job, I couldn't pay someone to take care of my mother and the kids."

"No, you're right. I'm just thinking about your options. When do you start getting Sam's unemployment?"

"Soon. But that will only be six hundred a month."

"How is Sam lately? I mean...towards you?"

Gretchen fought tears. "He...he doesn't mean to be cruel, I'm sure. It's just that..."

"You really need him now! Of course you do."

"Terry, men seem to...Sam seems to be able to turn love on and off. As if it were a matter of convenience. This is the worst time for me...and I can't reach him. He doesn't understand."

"I know. Do you still love him, Gretchen?" Terry asked quietly.

She stared down at her lap. "I don't know. I'll admit that I've wondered about that, lately. It's hard to love him when he's so mean to me. Also, well, he's not the same man I fell in love with."

"What do you mean?" Terry asked. A fly buzzed annoyingly about the room. The faint sound of the air conditioner hummed in the background.

Gretchen pulled at the handkerchief in her hand and raised her eyes. "He was so successful when I met him, so self-assured. Now...I try not to blame him for not having enough insurance, but sometimes I do. I feel real angry about it. If we'd had enough insurance money, maybe we could have rebuilt. Maybe we wouldn't even have had to let Sam's father know. I...we wouldn't be in this position. And I wouldn't be..."

"What is it?" Terry leaned forward.

"I feel so...abandoned by him! You know? Am I going to have to repeat this all my life, being abandoned by people? The kids and I...it doesn't feel like we're a family anymore. And that's all I ever wanted, was to be in a family. Now Sam is taking that away from me, and it makes me mad as hell. Jesus!" She clenched her teeth, her hands tight fists. "I wish there was something I could do, but he won't listen to me."

After a moment, Terry said, "I remember what that felt like, when John wanted out and our family started to fall apart. I'm sorry, Gretchen."

The women sat in silence for a few moments. Then Terry asked, "What do you think is going to happen?"

"I think we're going to lose the house, and the cars, and everything we have," Gretchen said flatly, admitting her worst fear. "And I don't know if Sam and I can stand it. I don't know."

"Your house is on the market. Has there been much interest in it?"

Gretchen shook her head. "No. People come to look sometimes. But nobody's buying right now. Three years ago the housing market was unbelievable. Now it's dead."

"Gretchen." Terry rose to sit beside her friend. "I know things seem hopeless now, but they're not. You'd be amazed at what ideas people come up with when they're in this kind of situation."

Gretchen smiled wryly. She knew there was nothing Terry could do for her, but appreciated her attempt to bolster her spirits. "Terry...I'm having these thoughts of...just running away."

"Well, I'm sure it's natural to think that..."

"The future looks terrible," Gretchen said. "My mother is going to die soon. Sam and I can barely talk anymore. And I'm going to have to let Rósa go."

"Oh, no," Terry said. "That's rotten. She's been so much help with your mother."

"I'm sad for Rósa! Taking care of my mother has helped her with her grief over her children. It doesn't seem fair...I feel so bad for her. But like everything else, there's nothing I can do. We simply can't afford a housekeeper now."

After a moment, Terry asked. "Do you still pray, Gretchen?"

Gretchen blew her nose, calmer now. "Yeah. But that hasn't helped. Maybe there isn't a god up there, like Sam always said. I don't know. It almost seems like...God loves people who make a lot of money, and that's not us anymore. Does that sound crazy?"

Terry shrugged. "No more crazy than some other aspects about religion. Have a little faith, though. If not in God, than in the belief that things have a way of working out. In ways you'd never expect. Believe me, I see it every day. Sometimes the answer is to just let go."

Gretchen nodded, clinging to hope. "There's something else."

Terry waited.

"It's about Luís."

"Gretchen." Terry smiled sagely. "A women having an affair when her marriage isn't going well is practically a cliche."

"I suppose so," Gretchen admitted. "But I think about him all the time. When I'm with him, I feel happy! In spite of everything. The only thing I look forward to lately is taking Rósa to her meeting. He's a wonderful man, Terry. He makes me laugh. He tells me I'm beautiful. That means so much to me, especially when Sam is practically ignoring me."

Terry sighed. "Sam isn't himself. Don't do something you'll regret for the rest of your life, Gretchen."

"I won't," she promised, but her words lacked conviction. She felt deeply sad. Toward Sam, and their estrangement. And because Luís had taken Sam's place in bringing her the comfort that she so desperately needed.

Chapter Eighteen

When she arrived home, Gretchen steeled herself and sought out Rósa.

"Rósa?" Gretchen entered the kitchen as Rósa prepared a tray for Carole–orange juice, toast and peach slices. Rósa tried often to tempt her mother's appetite, sometimes getting her to eat a little.

"Señora?" Rósa answered, wiping her hands on her apron. She waited, as if sensing the seriousness of Gretchen's presence. Surely, Rósa felt the tension in the Carey home, like a tightening band that had strangled the once abundant laughter and joy. But she never asked questions, concerning herself only with Carole.

"Rósa, I have to talk to you about something."

"Sí, Señora," she said, nodding.

"Mr. Carey...doesn't have a job right now, Rósa." She touched her forehead. Her head throbbed. "I don't have money to pay you. I'm afraid this will be your last day with us. I'm sorry." Gretchen ran her fingers through her hair. "I wish I could..." she stared out the window, then said in a low voice, "make this stop."

"I understand, Señora," Rósa said, picking up the tray. Her bosom looked heavy and matronly under her faded apron. A mother, Gretchen thought, but without children. And now without anyone to care for at all. No longer needed.

Rósa silently carried out the tray and Gretchen exhaled sharply, holding onto the wall. She had never imagined having to be so cruel. She felt part of a chain, helplessly tugged by the link on top of her to jerk the one beneath her. Sam had been fired, had practically fired her as his wife, and now she had fired Rósa. What next? Who else would be hurt?

Later in the day she found Sam in the living room, polishing the piano keys. "I wish I could get these two keys fixed," he said when he saw her, dragging the rag over the keys that were chipped and brown. "But I hate to see them replaced with plastic. Not that we can afford to fix them, anyway."

She sank into a chair. "I let Rósa go."

"Well, that's good."

The familiar anger began its slow simmer, with burning waves across her stomach. "She loves my mother. Taking care of her has helped Rósa to cope with her own grief."

"I suppose," he said grudgingly.

"Don't you feel anything toward Rósa, Sam?"

"Of course I do, Gretchen." He stopped polishing as he spoke. "But if she's in our boat, she's in a sinking ship."

He continued to work on the keys. She didn't mind being with him–she had become almost accustomed to his remoteness. At least he wasn't blatantly hostile today. It was as if his unemployment had become a raging monster that possessed him at times, terrorizing her and the children. At other times he seemed spent, mild and resigned, yet ever distant from her. Each phase came and passed, in this new rhythm of their lives.

"Any interviews coming up?" she asked hopefully.

"Nope," he said. "It's interesting, isn't it? I went from the top of the heap to the bottom, in a very short tumble. What's that song...'Nobody knows you when you're down and out?'"

"Maybe you should stop tumbling, Sam," she said quietly.

"I don't know how," he said, looking at her for the first time in days. "You don't know what it's like."

"You're right, Sam," she admitted. "I don't know what it's like."

"I always thought I could fix anything. Machines, computer programs. When I wrote programs, like my fuzzy logic application, I just worked with it until I got all the bugs out. Until it did exactly what I wanted it to."

"Bugs?"

"Errors. But I don't know how to fix this–I don't know how to get the bugs out of my life and get it back on track. Sometimes a program goes into an endless loop and spits out the same answers until you shut it off. There's no end until you stop it. That's how this feels."

"Helpless, you mean?" she asked, amazed that he had opened up to her.

"Yeah, helpless," he said with disgust. "I know how to fix something logical, but I don't have a clue how to keep going, stay strong, find answers when there don't seem to be any. I don't have a clue."

He threw down the rag and started to play a fast, lively tune. She listened for a few moments, grateful she hadn't had to answer. She thought about the recent past. So strong and secure, so absolute and impenetrable. Now it seemed an illusion, like the mightiest mountainside, which with one stone's throw dissolves into a raging avalanche.

❆ ❆ ❆

A few days later, Gretchen answered a knocking at the door. Rósa waited on the front porch.

"Rósa! I thought you understood–oh, my. Well, come in."

"I worry about your mother, Señora. How is she?"

"Oh, you're here to visit her?" Gretchen said with relief, not wanting to explain again that she no longer had a job for her. "She's a little worse, I think. She has pain...she's spending more days in bed. To be honest...she really misses you."

"I miss her, too. Maybe I check on her?"

"Of course! It will do her good to see you."

Rósa hurried into Carole's room, and Gretchen heard her mother's excited greeting. "Rósa! My stars, I'm glad to see you. Sit with me. It's been terrible without you. They don't know how to take care of me around here..."

Gretchen smiled. Her mother and Rósa had found a special friendship that benefited them both. Carole treated Rósa like a daughter, and Gretchen didn't begrudge the relationship. Carole and Rósa had no history. No resentment and wounds to heal. How simple it must be, she thought, that Rósa and her mother could love each other without the complications that she and

Carole shared. And why not? Time slipped away as Carole deteriorated. In her last days, let her be loved.

An hour later, Gretchen found Rósa in the kitchen, cleaning the counter.

"Rósa..." Gretchen began, but Rósa held up her hand in a silencing gesture.

"I have no other work on Wednesdays."

"But I can't pay you!"

"You pay me when you can. You have already paid me so much, in other ways. Now I help you."

"Oh, Rósa," Gretchen said, hugging her. "How did I get so lucky?"

"I am lucky to have you, and your mother and children," Rósa said, tears in her eyes. "You have become like my...family."

"I'm glad," Gretchen said, touched. "That we have helped you."

Rósa gazed at her with wisdom and understanding. "Señora. I know this is a terrible time for you. Sometimes what happens can make you want to die. I know." She took Gretchen's hands in her own. "But you are a good woman."

"Thank you, Rósa," Gretchen said awkwardly. Did trying to be a good person matter? she wondered. She had once thought it did. Now she felt like a severed leaf, battered along by an insidious wind. Regardless of how hard she tried to make the right decisions.

"I will take your mother some juice," Rósa said. "Then I will mop the floor in here and start on the laundry."

Gretchen began to protest, then changed her mind. Rósa's help felt like charity, and she was not used to accepting charity. Yet, she knew that Rósa wanted and needed to help. She had become overburdened and overwhelmed with the care of her mother and her children. She pushed aside her pride, grateful for Rósa's presence.

Was this the beginning of her dependence, she wondered? Surely, accepting help from others in the near, frightening future would never be as comfortable and safe as her reliance on Rósa, who understood better than anyone the losses of her life.

❇ ❇ ❇

The next evening, Carole asked to sit in the easy chair and read the children a book.

"...and the bunny ran back to his mommy in the bunny hole, and never went into the forest again," Carole read, closing the book.

"Are you going to die?" Julia asked.

Gretchen took a step toward Carole, but she gave her a silencing look. Although the children knew their grandmother was sick, Gretchen had decided not to tell them about her impending death until the time loomed close.

"Yes, I am," Carole answered.

Julia rocked with the motion of the chair. She had taken to wearing lacy tops and shorts, socks adorned with bows and sequins, and frilly barrettes in her hair. Bucky, recently toilet trained, wore only underwear covered with turtles. With matching grape stains remaining on their faces from earlier popsicles, the children resembled eccentric cartoon characters.

"Are you afraid?" Julia asked.

"No!" She put her arm around Julia and squeezed her. "Everybody dies." She withdrew her arm, shifting uncomfortably, and Gretchen knew her shoulder was hurting her. "Death is part of life."

"But your skin is going to fall off!"

"Oh, this isn't *my* skin," Carole said, pulling at the loose skin on her arm. "My body is like a shell. There's something else inside of me that's very alive, that will continue to live after I die."

"You mean your soul, in heaven?" Julia asked.

"Maybe. Or maybe it's the love that I feel for you."

"You're not scared?" Julia asked suspiciously.

"No, sugar. All living things die. It's normal. I'm more afraid of," she looked at Gretchen, "not living right now. We can't think about *dying*. We have to love each other right now, and say what we need to say to each other."

"But I don't want you to die," Julia said, close to tears.

"I know you don't, sugar. But after I die, my body will go back to the earth. Flowers will grow on top of me, the rain will wash me and thunder will roar above me. I'll be part of the world, forever. I like that." She turned her head to gaze into

Julia's uplifted face. "And let me tell you something, sugar, and you too, Bucky."

Bucky grinned at her coyly. Julia's mouth fell open in anticipation.

"Even after I'm dead, you'll still feel the love. Because my love for you is so big and so strong, nothing can ever stop it. You'll still feel my love, as if I'd never gone."

❄ ❄ ❄

"Sam?" Gretchen had been taking bottles down from the cupboard, searching for Carole's pain medication, when he came up silently behind her. "Is something the matter?"

Evening approached, and in the dimly-lit kitchen his appearance startled her. He had been unemployed for two months. He might have aged ten years, with the loose, gray skin under his eyes, and his hair pressed flat on one side from his afternoon nap, and the stubble of his beard. Half the time he wandered around the house in his bathrobe, a rolled newspaper in his hand.

"When is Rósa coming?" he asked curtly.

"She's coming Wednesday. Is there something...?"

"I wonder," he said, his eyes burning into her, frightening her, "if it's not too much trouble to ask, if you can *put these dishes in the dishwasher!*" With a sweep of his arm, he knocked the glasses off the counter.

Recoiling from his outburst, she winced at the breaking glasses. He had never treated her with such anger and violence, and the rage she saw in his eyes alarmed her. "Sam, are you mad at me about something?" she asked cautiously.

His expression froze, then he burst out with demonic laughter. "Am I mad about something?" he sneered. "You have no idea how many things I *don't get mad about*!"

"What?"

He gestured, making wide circles with his arms. "I've been home for months now, trying to find work," he shouted. "I don't get mad at the mess I see around me everyday that piles up until Rósa shows up. I don't get mad at the way you and your mother and Rósa sit around all day and stop the conversation whenever I come into the room. I don't get mad at the fact that *you*"–he pointed at her maliciously–"run off with those kids to the park, and to birthday parties, and to friend's houses, and when it's dinner time I'm scrounging through the refrigerator for a tuna fish sandwich! Goddamn it, Gretchen. I'm sick and tired of not getting mad about this situation."

"What, Sam? What?" she retorted. "I spend time with my mother, who's going to die within a month, probably. I play with the kids. You barely even know they exist anymore. Do you notice their faces, when they see you? They've become afraid of you!" A last ray of sunlight streamed through the kitchen window, striking her face, and her green eyes shimmered with tears. "Maybe I'm not trying hard to be a good wife lately. I'm sorry." Her gaze beseeched him, and the hardness of his expression softened.

"You're home all day, every day," she said, starting to cry. "You don't talk to me, except to criticize. You don't touch me anymore. I'm sorry you can't find a job. I know what that's doing to you. But I'm hurting too, Sam. We're going to lose the house, and I don't know where we're going to go. I need you, and you're not really here. Can't we just..."

He turned and left the room. She reached out to him silently, started to say something, then changed her mind. As devastating as it felt for him to walk away, it had become commonplace. She couldn't reach him, no matter how hard she tried. His rejection no longer shocked her. Each day, she walked around in the wake of his distance.

She gazed out the window. The sun had almost set completely over the western valley. It had leached the light from the sky, giving her neighborhood the appearance of a black-and-white photo. She waited for the comfort of darkness, the blackness of her dreamless sleep, the light having been snuffed out of her own life as well.

Chapter Nineteen

On Thursday of the next week, at eight o'clock at night, the phone rang and Gretchen ran to pick it up. "Hello?"

"This is Dr. Myers."

"Dr. Myers." Gretchen gripped the receiver. "Thank you for calling me back. My mother's having a lot of pain."

Silence. "Well. That's to be expected. Maybe you should make an appointment, then."

Gretchen fought off the suspicion that he didn't want to help her. "Tomorrow? Can I bring her in tomorrow?"

"Call the office in the morning."

"But what do I do about tonight?" she asked desperately.

After another silence, he said, "What's the number of your pharmacy? I'll call in a prescription."

After she hung up, she gave the children a bath and put them to bed. Then she looked in the study, and found Sam staring at his computer screen. She decided against disturbing him. She drove alone in the night to pick up her mother's medicine. When she returned, her mother had fallen into a fitful sleep.

In her bedroom, she took the papier-maché elephants and tigers off her dresser and fingered them lovingly, finding comfort in her art. Tomorrow she would start a new project, she decided, something big to take her mind off her problems. Maybe a piñata for Julia's fifth birthday in November. She would make a rhino, or better yet, an elephant. For the first time in months, she went to sleep with something to look forward to.

The next morning, she called Dr. Myers office. After pressuring his receptionist, she arranged for an appointment at eleven o'clock.

She had given her mother a dose of her new medication when she woke up, and helped her into her clothes as they prepared to leave.

"Does the new medicine help, Mother?"

"A little," Carole said, and Gretchen could tell she was in pain. "Brush my hair, will you sugar?"

Gretchen sat behind Carole on her bed and made gentle strokes with her mother's soft brush. She glanced at Carole's face in the mirror and saw the eyes closed and almost bluish, the pasty skin, the cheekbones sharply protruding.

Impulsively, she wrapped her arms around her mother and kissed her on the cheek. "I love you," she said gently.

Her mother's face took on the expression of a madonna: the love for her child, the suffering, the resignation and yet the will to keep on living came through in the tilt of her head, the set of her mouth, the frail hands that clutched Gretchen's arms as they held her in an embrace.

If Gretchen's faith in God had wavered, it returned with the surge of love she felt for her mother, and the power and strength of her love. The past seemed to fall away and the moment was glorious, perfect in its fulfillment. She closed her eyes, trying not to think, basking in this moment of contentment.

❄ ❄ ❄

Dr. Myers took a chest x-ray, then conferred with Gretchen and Carole. "There's a tumor growing in her shoulder," he said to Gretchen, as if Carole weren't there.

Carole hunched over on the table, rubbing her shoulder protectively with her eyes closed.

"Well, we need to talk about a stronger pain medication," Gretchen said.

He glanced at Carole's x-ray. Bulky in his white coat, he had always reminded her of a butcher. "The medicine I gave her is pretty strong."

"But she's still having pain! And it's only going to get worse."

He gave her a dismissive look. "Mrs. Carey. Everyone has pain."

She had been continually offended by his disregard for her mother. By his callous statements in Carole's presence, and his seeming indifference to her care and treatment plan. But this last statement seemed unforgivable, an inexcusable admission of his apathy toward Carole that she could not ignore. Her temper, already close to the surface lately, snapped.

"Dr. Myers. You may be right. But I think people with cancer probably have more pain than you or I do. I don't care what that x-ray says, or even what you think anymore. My mother is having pain, or she wouldn't complain about it!"

She thought she saw him roll his eyes. "You are an arrogant, insensitive man," she lashed out at him. "You have no interest in my mother because she's old." She glanced at Carole and saw a slight smile on her lips, so she continued. "And terminal. We just aren't big enough bucks for you, are we Dr. Myers? We've refused your attempts to put her in the hospital. Or to put her through tests and procedures and treatments that would benefit only your *wallet*!"

He smirked. "Gretchen, you don't know what–"

"Donald," she said with contempt, addressing him in the familiar as well, "you are FIRED! You have not done a good job in regards to my mother, and your services are no longer needed."

He laughed nervously. "But what–"

Carole got off the table and Gretchen steadied her. "I don't know, I don't know! But there must be a doctor in Los Angeles who has a little compassion. Who will treat my mother like a human being, with dignity, not like an...insurance payment! Who will have an inkling of how her illness is affecting our family. And you, Doctor, are not that man. Goodbye."

"Don't forget to pay for the visit at the front desk," he called after her coldly.

She turned back and faced him. "I can't pay now. My husband is unemployed. Her insurance will pay most of the bill, then we'll have to work out the rest."

Without another word to him, she led Carole from the office. She felt such elation, such satisfaction in finishing with him, it was as if he no longer existed for her.

"I didn't know you had so much gumption," Carole said as they drove home. "His jaw looked like it was about to drop on the floor."

"Well, I never did," Gretchen said, delighted. "But it's funny. Lately I think I've been building some character. It's like...I have nothing to lose. Things are so bad already. And I just couldn't stand for him to treat you like that. When we get home I'll call Terry. She'll know of a doctor, I'm sure. Don't worry."

"I'm not worried, sugar. It's a big relief not to have to see that doctor again."

"I don't want you to suffer, Mother. I don't want you to be mistreated."

Carole gripped Gretchen's hand weakly. "I don't know why you're being so good to me. After what I put you through when you were a little girl, I wonder that you don't hate me."

Gretchen recognized the extraordinary moment: this was her chance, if she took it. For an instant, she wanted to berate her mother for abandoning her. She was tempted to vent the full extent of the anger she had harbored over the years as a child, buried, then rediscovered at times during her mother's stay. She could cruelly reject her, in vindication of herself, Ted and her father, for the hardship she had caused them.

Since the day her mother arrived, Gretchen had been consumed with her illness. The issue of her own lost years had been shoved aside. Even during her mother's confession and revelations, she had focused on Carole's tragedy and pain, but never on her own. She could understand what had happened to her mother, but what about *her*?

She saw her mother's trusting face, and the guilt etched into the wrinkled, anxious expression. This is a woman who has suffered enough, she thought. Can I tell her about my own pain, without destroying her? I'll never have another chance.

"Mom..." She couldn't believe she had called her that. The word had slipped out. Yet it felt tender, poignant, especially in light of her mother's fading life. "I don't want to hurt you. And I...empathize with what happened to you. I'm married now, and things aren't going so well." She choked, then steadied herself, determined to finish.

"But I wonder if you can understand how hard it was for me." She paused, her emotions rising. "You took away my childhood," she blurted out suddenly, angrily, as clear as she had ever been in her life. "I heard about this mess of your past and I felt sad. But what about me and Ted? While you were feeling sorry for yourself, we were growing up without a mother. I didn't even know how to dress myself, or...or how to fix my hair. Dad was so lonely. You say he ran you out, but it killed him, whatever happened. I spent my childhood trying to make him happy. All my friends had mothers and Ted and I would come home from school every day to an empty house. Dad would get home from work and we barely knew what to say to each other. For years! I felt...left behind, by both you and Dad."

She had reached her neighborhood, and pulled to the curb. Her confession left her purged, weightless. With sudden concern, she looked at her mother, who smiled at her lovingly.

"Mother...I didn't mean to...are you all right?"

Carole shook her head. "You are absolutely right. Every word. And do you know how it makes me feel to hear you? Honored. That you can tell me the truth. Because if it helps you, sugar, for me to hear how it was for you, then I'm glad. We don't have much more time to talk about it. This is it. I want you to get everything off your chest."

"But...I don't want to hurt you. I just..."

"You want me to know how much I hurt you. And you should. Because my leaving was important, it affected your whole life. We can't just sweep it under the rug as if it never happened, or didn't matter."

Gretchen hugged her, filled with gratitude.

"I just want to know–can you really forgive me?" Her mother's face was open and vulnerable, waiting.

Gretchen's lip trembled. "I can. I really can. When you first came back I resented you, especially because you wouldn't tell me why you left."

"I was so scared. So ashamed."

"I know. But I've come to really love you. When you told me about why you left...about the baby and how you lost it, I couldn't blame you."

Carole bowed her head at the mention of her dead daughter, and Gretchen could see her pain. Her deep, terrible sorrow.

"I know what it means to be a mother," Gretchen said quietly. "The fear of losing a child...I can't judge you, Mother. Of course I forgive you. Why should I waste what time we have left with anger? The past is over."

Weakly, Carole reached out and took Gretchen's hand. "I'm proud that you're my daughter," she said. "And I'm so glad I found you."

"Me too," Gretchen said. "I'm glad I found you, too."

❄ ❄ ❄

She drove home, and helped her mother settle in her room for a nap. Then she called Terry.

After recounting what had happened, Gretchen said, "So, I'm wondering if you know a good doctor."

"Gretchen, I am so relieved you got rid of that doctor. And yes, I do. One of my clients has cancer, and has been seeing Doctor Byerly, in Encino. She says Doctor Byerly is very compassionate. The kind of doctor you would want for your mother. And he makes house calls."

"Wonderful," Gretchen said. "I'll get his number from the book and call him."

"Good. I know this is a difficult time for you, Gretchen. I think you'll find it much more bearable with a good doctor you can communicate with."

"I hope so," Gretchen said, unable to imagine what that meant. Quickly, she told Terry about her conversation with her mother.

"Oh, Gretchen. You are so lucky. I'm so happy for you."

"I know," Gretchen said, still glowing from the experience.

"Most people don't have a chance to make peace with their parents before they die. They live the rest of their lives thinking, 'If only I had said this, or that. If only we'd talked about our relationship.'"

"Well, I feel lucky then. I got everything off my chest, and didn't hold back. And the best thing was, she listened and accepted what I said."

"I think you had a lot of courage to tell her."

"Thanks," Gretchen said. "Lately I've gotten braver."

"How are things...?"

"Tense. We started getting Sam's unemployment, but our savings aren't going to last long."

Terry sighed on the other end. "Hang in there, Gretchen. I know it's hard."

"Thanks, Terry," Gretchen said quietly. "You're a good friend."

She took the children to a birthday party, and when she returned she called Dr. Byerly's office and made an appointment for her mother. She felt enormously uplifted to be rid of Dr. Myers, and to be more in control of her mother's situation.

She looked for Sam, then remembered he had a job interview today. Each time he went out she felt cautiously optimistic. Maybe this time... But she had started to believe that finding work was impossible for him. Not that it was his fault. Times were bad. News of layoffs dominated the paper. What scared her most, though, was that he seemed to be giving up. He went out on fewer and fewer interviews, as if he thought finding a job had become futile.

Sadly, she had to admit she felt relieved when he wasn't home. Clearly, they had become estranged. Without a word, Gretchen had begun sleeping in her mother's room. Sam never mentioned the change, and she suspected he felt as relieved as she did. He avoided her now, and rarely spoke to her. It was as if his life had become a permanent, bitter sulk. She was too overwhelmed with her children, and her mother's care, to try harder at patching their relationship.

Their dwindling resources, and the bills that remained unpaid haunted her daily. At times she managed to switch off her thoughts. She concentrated instead on her mother, and her children, and increasingly in her daydreams, Luís.

She went into the garage. All day, she had looked forward to starting Julia's piñata. Life couldn't stop because they were going broke. She would make the piñata and fill it with candy. She would give Julia a party in the park with Lorie and a few of her school friends, that wouldn't cost much money. Julia would have something to look forward to, now that she knew her grandmother was dying, and understood that her father was out of work.

She made a frame with chicken wire, then cut out strips of newspaper. She made her paste–a mixture of corn starch, flour, and diluted white glue. She dipped the newspaper strips into the paste and draped them carefully over the frame.

Next, she found a package of balloons on the shelf that she kept for her papier-maché projects. She blew up a long one, for the nose, and attached it to the frame. She covered the balloon with the newspaper strips. When they dried and hardened, she would use a pin to pop the balloon.

She checked her watch. She would have to pick up the children soon. When she had a chance, she would make the ears, feet and a tail for her creation. Then when her elephant had dried completely, she would paint it gray and glue on strips of colored paper.

She loved elephants. She loved their magnificence and their intelligence. If her own life had gone bad, then she took heart that the poaching of African elephants had declined since they were declared an endangered species last year. Someday, she prayed, they would be completely out of danger. The greed for ivory would somehow be extinguished.

Chapter Twenty

A few days later, Gretchen approached Sam cautiously in the backyard. Untended, the crab grass had spread, strangling the once-lush lawn. Weeds grew high to the fence. "Sam?" she said.

He ignored her. Sitting in a dusty lawn chair, he wore blue shorts and a wrinkled blue T-shirt, his feet bare. He had shaved a week ago. The blond stubble on his face had turned soft, the beginning of a beard.

"Sam," she said quietly. "A notice of foreclosure came today. The bank is selling the house next month unless we can make the payment."

He shrugged. "I guess that's it, then."

"What are we supposed to do?" she asked, exasperated.

"I don't know. You figure it out," he said, refusing to look at her.

She waited a moment. "You want me to figure it out. I have a dying mother in there, and two kids. And now you want me to figure this out."

He gave her a challenging stare, shielding the sun from his eyes with his hand. "If your mother hadn't come, maybe we wouldn't be in this situation. If I hadn't had to pay for her medical bills, I could have started over."

"You blame my *mother* for this situation?" she finally sputtered. "How dare you! What kind of a man are you? Jesus," she said through clenched teeth. "You didn't take out enough insurance. You allowed the building to burn down, and–"

He sprang to his feet. "Gretchen, don't!" he warned, pointing his finger at her in a threatening gesture.

After months of not getting any reaction from him at all, she egged him on. "And now you put the blame on a dying woman," she said, eyes flashing, hands on her hips. "Maybe your father was right. Maybe you are irresponsible. A loser."

His face turned a gray shade of white. Like ashes from white paper, she thought. Or ice. She knew she had gone too far. He gripped her arm.

"You're hurting me!" she protested as his fingers dug into her flesh.

"Don't you ever, ever call me that again," he said, his voice low, his eyes full of hate. "I am not a loser! I am a..."

"Let go of me," she demanded, meeting his gaze.

She ripped her arm from his grasp. She struggled to catch her breath. Her eyes swept over him contemptuously. "You'd better find someone else to blame. Here," she tossed the bank notice at his feet. "Read it yourself. Maybe if you're not too busy you can help us figure something out."

She walked away from him, into the house. At that moment, she didn't care if she ever saw him again.

❄ ❄ ❄

One morning during the next week, Gretchen made herself a cup of coffee and reached for the sugar bowl.

"Damn," she muttered, finding it empty. "I forgot to buy more at the store."

"Rósa!" she yelled. "I'm going next door to borrow some sugar."

As she climbed the steep stairway on the side of Paula's house, she heard voices from the porch.

"...I know the market is terrible, but it's still hard to get into a house." Paula's voice came clearly to Gretchen's ears. "I'm just saying that the house next door is going to be repossessed. You can probably pick it up cheap at the sale."

Gretchen stood stock still, listening. "How can you be so sure?" a man's voice followed.

Paula laughed. "My neighbor is out of work. He used to be big in defense, but that's all over now. He hangs around the house all the time. I can hear him playing the piano. His wife's just an Oakie. A housewife. They thought they were better than everyone else, but now..."

Gretchen fled back to her house, tears of humiliation burning her eyes, her heart pounding with panic.

❄ ❄ ❄

Later in the week, Dr. Byerly arrived to meet Carole. "Mrs. Simpson?" Dr. Byerly entered Carole's bedroom and she tried to rise from her bed.

"Here, let me help you," he said, gently taking her arm and easing her back in bed. He appeared to be a youthful forty. He wore a dress shirt and tie, and dark slacks, as if he had come from the hospital. On his feet, he wore running shoes. He had a smile and easy manner that engaged Gretchen immediately. This, she thought, is a doctor I can trust.

"How have you been feeling?" he asked Carole.

"Kind of crummy. My shoulder's been hurting more. I don't think the medicine the other doctor gave me is working anymore."

"She moans in the night," Gretchen said. "She has a lot of pain between doses."

"Okay," Dr. Byerly said. "Then we need to address the pain. My feeling is, keeping you comfortable is most important."

Gretchen was struck by the way he talked *to* her mother, and not as if she were an object in the room, or a child.

"I saw your last x-ray, the one Dr. Myers took." He put his hands behind his back, and faced Carole squarely. Gretchen had opened the blinds earlier, and the bright August sun illuminated the room. Bucky, Julia and Lorie crowded in the doorway, watching Dr. Byerly.

"The cancer is definitely spreading. I saw a good-sized tumor in your lung. I think it got knocked down by radiation for a while, but now it's back." He talked frankly, clearly, and Carole nodded her head as he spoke.

"I know there's nothing more you can do," Carole said, a little loudly.

"Well, there is," he said, and his smile conveyed his

knowledge and expertise of his business, cancer. "You do have choices. You can get more radiation. We can try chemotherapy. But I believe you know already that those options won't extend your life very much, and certainly not the quality of your life."

"No," Carole said morosely, staring down at her sheets.

"But that's up to you, and your family. I will do whatever you want me to do."

"I don't want to go through any more of that," Carole said. "I know I'm dying, and I don't have much time left. If you can keep me from being in so much pain," her eyes begged him, "then I'd be grateful."

"Okay," Dr. Byerly said. "Let's talk about our plan. First, we need to get you a hospital bed. I'll contact the hospice organization at our hospital and have them arrange for that. And speaking of hospice, I think it would be a good idea to get them involved. They can send a nurse over here three times a week, at least, to help with your care. They have other services as well, such as counseling and child care, if that's something you need. "Now, let's get your pain under control. I'm going to call a pharmaceutical company we use and have them set you up with a morphine pump."

Carole and Gretchen stared at him blankly.

"They'll insert a small needle in your leg, and you'll get a continuous dose of morphine. No more pills wearing off in the middle of the night.

"Hospice will take over most of your care, but I'll be available if you have any questions or if you decide you want any more treatments. I'll check on you once a week."

"My mother's insurance won't cover the whole bill..."

Dr. Byerly gave her a well-rehearsed smile. "Everyone is in debt of some kind. The hospital will make an arrangement with you to pay the rest over time. Don't let that worry you now."

"My housekeeper is used to caring for my mother."

"She won't be displaced. We want to help you, not upset your routine. Mrs. Simpson, do you have any questions?"

"No," Carole said. "Let's get on with it."

As Gretchen saw Dr. Byerly to the door, she said, "I can't tell you how much better I feel that you've come, Doctor. I appreciate your kindness...now things seem more under control."

He followed her down the hall. "Oh, I'm a doctor who feels that dying patients should be treated with dignity. There's no reason for her to suffer, if we can help it."

"Can you really stop the pain, especially as the cancer advances?" Gretchen asked anxiously. She didn't want to seem so harried...she knew she had dark circles under her eyes, and she had lost weight. She and Sam had barely spoken since the incident in the backyard, and the strain wore on her. She thought she looked terrible.

He touched her shoulder in a comforting way as they stepped into the foyer. "I'll be honest with you. It might get kind of rough at the end. Sometimes a cancer patient has a sharp increase in pain as the disease spreads. It takes a while for us to catch up with the medication. But, we'll do everything we can for her."

"Thank you, Doctor," Gretchen said, her eyes glistening.

"Mrs. Carey." He touched her shoulder again, this time firmly. "You seem like a woman who can use support. Taking care of a dying parent at home is very stressful. You need more help. I don't mean to imply you can't handle it. Clearly you can. But I think you'll find that hospice will make your life much easier. I know life can't be easy now."

"I've...tried to do the right thing for her," Gretchen said. She saw him to his car. She could not have imagined her relief at his help, and the sheer tiredness she felt now that the responsibility for her mother would be shared. Rósa helped as much as she could, as a friend, but had to take other jobs to support herself. Some weeks she only came one or two days, leaving Gretchen with the brunt of the care. She feared that Rósa indeed would feel left out, replaced by a regular nurse. But she was determined that would not happen; Rósa had healed so much over the months since her children had died.

She took her mother a high-calorie drink–practically the only food she would take now–and checked on the children. Julia had turned on the Wizard of Oz in the den. Lorie nestled between her and Bucky on the couch.

"Lorie's my friend!" Bucky yelled.

"She's *my* friend!" Julia shouted back.

"Lorie is *both* your friend," Gretchen said, with as much authority as she could muster. Her varying roles as a parent seemed endless, and more complicated lately.

She made the children a big bowl of microwave popcorn, then went into the garage. She prepared her starch and glue mixture, and it felt cool and slippery to her fingers as she dipped her newspaper strips. The foreclosure notice from the bank had been placed in the bill holder, with all the other unpaid bills. Time is running out, she thought, and we have no plan. Right now, I have four hundred dollars in the checking account. Nothing in savings. Our credit cards are almost at their limit.

She sat on the stool next to the elephant, carefully applying the strips to the cardboard ears. Any day, my car will be repossessed. What little money I have left, I have to save for groceries. She laid down the paper strips, smoothing them with her hands. There is no more hope. No more delusions. We are sinking into poverty.

Yet, as her life deteriorated day be day, all she could think about was her mother. Her mother's last days, of which she played an unexpected part. She wouldn't have missed this time, as Ted had chosen to do. The last time I will ever spend with my mother, she thought. Which feels like the first and the best time, which feels like a gift.

❆ ❆ ❆

Late in the night, Gretchen woke with a start.

"Mommy, Mommy!"

It took her a moment to clear her head from sleep–she was in her mother's room, in the spare bed. Where she slept now.

"Mommy!" she heard, then the sound of crying.

It was Julia, screaming for her. She dashed into Julia's room. Her bed was empty. Where was she? Gretchen heard her daughter cry again. The sound came from her and Sam's bedroom.

Sam sat up on his side of the bed, in his pajamas. He had turned on his reading light. Julia, huddled on the floor, cried hysterically.

"What happened?" Gretchen demanded, hurrying to her daughter.

"Daddy...Daddy pushed me out of bed," Julia sobbed. "He hit me with his elbow." She clung to Gretchen, her cheeks wet with tears.

"Sam?" Gretchen said, her wrath starting to build. "What happened?"

"She must have come into bed with me earlier. All I know is that she woke me up. She was kicking me. I asked her to stop. She kicked me again and I pushed her out of bed."

"I had a bad dream," Julia wailed. "I dreamed I was dead."

Gretchen stood up, completely awake now. She strode over to Sam with fists clenched. "How could you knock her out of bed?" she demanded. "She could have hurt herself. How could you do such a thing?"

"I...I," he acted like he wanted to explain, then his face changed. He glared at Julia, then at Gretchen, his cheeks red.

"Goddamn it," he shouted. "I can't stand it! This *kid*"–he pointed at Julia accusingly–"tortures me at night. I want her out of this room. I don't want her coming in here anymore. Do you understand, Julia?"

Julia cried harder. She pushed herself into a cross-legged position, her thin cotton nightie bunched around her lap.

"Julia has nightmares," Gretchen tried to stay calm. "She needs reassurance, not...getting thrown out of bed."

"Then let her sleep with you!" Sam yelled.

"I would have," Gretchen retorted. "But she got in bed with *you*. You're her father. She doesn't understand that...that I'm not sleeping in here now," she said in a low voice.

Sam stared at the floor. "Get her out of here," he said curtly.

Gretchen had tolerated his coldness toward her. His moodiness and outbursts, bordering on abuse. But there was no way she would allow him to mistreat Julia. He had gone too far. Something inside of her snapped, and her rage toward him spilled out. "Don't you ever talk about our daughter like that," she screamed at him. "If you don't love me anymore, fine. But she's still your daughter!"

With an expression of annoyance on his face, he got up and pushed her into the wall. "Goddamn you," he muttered through his teeth, eyes glazed. "She's a spoiled brat. Thanks to you. Don't try to manipulate me."

She found her footing, dazed. Julia crept into the corner, still crying. Her tear-stained face looked terrified. And heartbroken, as if she had lost everything. Gretchen would never forget that look.

"Why don't you just leave?" Gretchen said with icy finality, rubbing her arm where it had struck the wall. "Please. We don't want you here anymore." The perfect family. The perfect life. Thoughts from such a short time before echoed in her mind, tormenting her. Now her life lay shattered, irreparable. All she wanted was for him to leave.

But the request seemed to enrage him further. He rose from the bed and stormed toward her. "You want *me* to leave! This is still *my* house, goddamn it. You did not contribute one penny. I have had it with your demands, your complaints and your whining." In the dim light the expression on his face appeared crazed, igniting her fear. He grabbed her wrist and pulled her out of the bedroom.

"Is everything all right?" Gretchen heard her mother call weakly from her room.

"No!" Sam roared, dragging Gretchen down the hall.

"Mommy?" she heard Bucky's tentative voice.

"Sam. Stop it." She clawed at his hand on her wrist.

He opened the front door. "You leave, you ungrateful bitch. See how far you can get on your own." He pushed her out on the porch and slammed the door behind her.

She blinked in the cool air, stunned. Then her bravery crumbled and she slumped against the door. "Sam," she cried. "You have to let me in. The children. Open the door, Sam. Please."

She pounded on the door. It was as if the house had become a fortress against her as she begged to be let in. Minutes passed like hours. Tears blinded her eyes.

Suddenly, the door opened and Sam reached for her. "Oh, God. I'm so sorry. How could I do such a thing? I'm so sorry. I'm so sorry. Please forgive me."

He held her in his arms and she sagged against him, grateful only that the nightmarish scene was over. Through the door she heard the crying of her children. Her mother calling her name.

"What's happening to us, Sam?" she whispered, for a moment feeling like she had him back.

"I don't know, honey. I didn't mean..."

"But why...?"

He lifted his head. "I'm being swallowed up. That's how it feels. Drowning. Suffocating. Dying. It's making me crazy, I know. I don't mean to hurt you, or the kids. Oh my God, Julia." He gave her one last embrace, then rushed into the house to his daughter.

"It's okay, Mother. I'll be right there," she called wearily to Carole.

She leaned against the door frame, exhausted, her emotions spent. How could this be happening to them? She had once thought her family to be immune to hardship. Now ugliness encroached on their lives like a menacing spider.

Then it struck her. This is what I've read about happening in other people's homes. With other people. The loss of income. The lack of money. The violence and desperation. The despair. The abuse and screaming.

But not us, she thought, a sob breaking in her throat. Not us. This can't be happening to us.

Chapter Twenty One

So, do you go to shooting galleries a lot?" Terry asked loudly.

Gretchen slid the last round into the chamber and pushed in the cylinder, giving it a playful twirl. She grinned. "Shooting galleries are places for dope addicts. We call this a firing range. I come once in a while to keep my skills up."

"And to blow off steam?"

"Yeah," Gretchen said. She lay the gun on the shelf and clipped her first target, a silhouette of a man's torso, onto the pulley. She pressed the button on the wall and the pulley carried the target into the firing range until she stopped it at about twenty feet.

Gretchen picked up the nickel-plated, .38 special, gripping the ivory handles. She wore her ear muffs like a hairband, and her auburn hair fell like scalloped waves away from her face and down the back of her neck. She had dressed in clothing reminiscent of her days in Oklahoma, when life had been so much simpler: old blue jeans with holes in the knees, a plain white T-shirt, and her lizard-skin cowboy boots.

"Want to give it a try?" Gretchen yelled, but Terry shook her head.

"I can't imagine firing a gun! I've never seen this side of you before. Don't you feel strange, with all these men?"

Gretchen gave her a humoring smile. Her friend had agreed to accompany her, but now seemed conspicuously out of place. She had dressed in a bright blue jumpsuit and pumps, and stood with her arms crossed tightly against her chest. She kept glancing nervously through the yellow-filmed glass that separated the firing range from the smoky lobby, where men in baseball caps passed by and occasionally stared at the women.

Gretchen crouched slightly, feet spread, and fired a round dead-center into the head of the target. "These old boys? Naw. They're just like the men from home I used to shoot with."

"Oh. There's sort of a club, then, of people who shoot guns for fun?"

Gretchen cocked the lever and fired, ripping a hole in the center of the target. The smell of gunpowder filled her nostrils. "Only club I ever belonged to," she yelled, and suddenly felt so at home in the range, and yet so painfully homesick for Oklahoma, that she fired the next three rounds in quick succession, striking the target off-center. She hit the button, unclipped the target, and attached another one. It was a picture of a would-be mugger, with a stocking over his head, pointing a gun at her. She pushed the button, and the poster glided away.

"Are you okay?" Terry asked. "You seem so...intense."

"I'm okay," Gretchen answered, her own voice muffled and flat to her ears. "I just..."

She looked away. She flipped out the cylinder, ejected the shells and reloaded. "I can't live this way, Terry," she said softly.

"What?" Terry shouted, holding her ear muffs and screwing up her face.

"I can't live with him!" Gretchen screamed.

Terry stepped back, as if shocked by either the noise or the revelation. "What are you going to do?" She glanced behind her at the window, and two unshaven rednecks smiled at her good-naturedly. She moved closer into the stall.

Gretchen fired three quick rounds, blowing holes in the chest of the mugger. She jerked back the lever. She had begun to sweat. "I'm thinking about taking the kids to Oklahoma."

"Really?" Terry said, her expression puzzled. "What about your mom?"

"After my mom...dies," she said brutally. She fired again, hitting the mugger between the eyes.

"Boy," Terry said, as if mulling over the idea. "Are things really that bad?"

"Things are that bad," Gretchen said between her teeth, not knowing if Terry heard her. She lowered the gun. A pot-bellied, grizzled man carrying a .45 passed the stall, then stopped and smiled at Gretchen. She stared back, stone-faced, and he quickly moved on.

"Things aren't going to get better, Terry. He's not even looking for a job anymore. We don't talk at all. The tension's so thick that–"

"But what will you do in Oklahoma?"

Gretchen ejected the used shells and slid new rounds into the chambers. "I don't know! Start a new life. My dad will help me. Look," Her face was only inches from Terry's. Shots from the other stalls permeated the air, and she waited for a lull in the din. "I've tried to reach him. I've tried to be understanding."

She leaned her back against the brown, padded wall. "I can't change Sam. I don't know him anymore. And you know what?"

Terry waited.

She changed her target, and the new poster was of a full-sized, clean-cut looking man. She emptied five shots, in rapid succession, into the figure's crotch.

"My God," Terry yelled, staring at the target. She held her hands over her ear muffs, as if to shield herself from the noise, or the presence of guns, or the violence. "What were you going to say?"

Gretchen set down the gun and turned toward Terry. "Sam doesn't have any balls. He's a coward. When the going gets tough, Sam plays the piano. Lately, I can't even respect him."

She felt too drained, too exhausted, to even cry. She simply felt empty. Her mother would be dead soon. Her life, as she had known it with Sam, was dead too. She had to accept the truth and move on.

"I'm so sorry, Gretchen," Terry said with anguish. "I'll miss you so much."

Gretchen gave her a resigned smile. "I know. I'm sorry it's worked out this way. But I can't handle this anymore." She pressed the button, drawing in the bullet-riddled target.

Terry seemed to consider for a moment. "What about Luís?" she yelled.

Her emotions raw, Gretchen clipped on the next target, barely glancing at it. Her body suddenly felt hollow, bruised. "You can't have everything you want, Terry. Some things aren't meant to be."

"But, Gretchen!"

She raised the gun. "I'll get over him. I've gotten good at getting over things. You know?"

She spread her legs and peered down the barrel. "Jesus Christ!"

The new target displayed a tiny hunter, dressed in red and carrying a sports rifle, drawing a bead on a large, full-tusked, charging elephant. Concentric bull's-eye circles had been drawn on the side of the elephant's face.

"Can you believe this?" Gretchen said in disgust. With grim determination, she fired all five rounds into the hunter, completely tearing the image from the poster.

"Pretty good shooting."

She turned to see two men watching her, both wearing baseball caps, dark glasses, and ear muffs. The shorter one had on a shirt imprinted with a skull and the words, "Soldiers for Supremacy".

"Thanks," she said, a little warily. Terry gave her an anxious glance.

"You didn't hit the real target, though," the shorter one laughed. "You need to move your gun over about six inches."

The other man, long-faced and with thinning, dark hair, laughed uproariously. "That's right, lady," he sputtered, nudging his friend. "You need a good six inches."

Terry shrunk back. Gretchen lay her gun on the shelf and faced the men. She pulled herself up tall, her T-shirt wet with sweat, her green eyes dauntless. "Boys," she said curtly. "Like I was telling my friend a few minutes ago. These days, a good six inches just doesn't cut it."

Chapter Twenty Two

Near the end of August, her mother lay in her hospital bed, her back propped up by several pillows. "Is that better, Mother?" Gretchen asked. The nurse had left a few minutes earlier, after giving Carole a bath.

"Wonderful," her mother said weakly. She seemed to grow thinner every day. She could no longer get out of bed. A catheter bag hung from the cold steel bed rail. A plastic case about the size of a cigarette pack that contained a week's supply of morphine lay on the bed, and pumped the medicine continually into Carole's leg through a needle.

The room had been turned into a high-tech, miniature hospital room, all for her mother's care and comfort. She emitted a heavy, sweet odor, even after she was bathed, and other odors of betadyne, lemon glycerine and hospital soap hung in the air. Death smells, Gretchen thought as she wearily took her place in the chair next to her mother's bed. And smells to mask the odor of death.

She spent every available moment next to her mother's bed. Her children and Sam had taken on a distant existence. Sam had been subdued lately. Less hostile, but still distant. As if simply embarrassed by his behavior during the night of Julia's nightmare. She had forgiven him, she supposed, but she remained wary. And she would never forget how he had treated her and Julia. She would bide her time, and if nothing had changed after her mother died, she would take the kids and move to Oklahoma.

Sam had left this morning without a word, as he often did. She had stopped wondering where he went long ago.

She cared for her children efficiently, gave them what they needed, only wanting to return to her mother's room. If Carole woke, she wanted to be there for her, holding her hand.

"Are you afraid, Mother?" she asked, wiping Carole's forehead with a moist towel.

"Yes," her mother said, and Gretchen searched for reassuring words. Tumors protruded visibly from her shoulders and back, and under her knees. Probably, Dr. Byerly had said last week during his visit, the disease had spread to her liver and brain.

"I'll stay with you, Mom. I won't leave you. You aren't alone ," Gretchen said. The love and forgiveness she felt for her mother were a partial salve on her grief.

After Carole had fallen asleep, Gretchen went to the kitchen for some coffee. Even with the help of the nurse who came three times a week and Rósa, she still felt mentally and physically exhausted. Drained from worry and loss, she thought. And from the work of letting go of my mother.

The bills piled up. Paying the mortgage was out of the question. They would lose the house. Her mother's medical bills piled up as well, and she could only hope they could pay them off someday in the future. Financial pressures seemed less important now, with the death of her mother so close.

The doorbell rang as she poured her coffee, followed by continuous knocking. At twelve in the afternoon, she couldn't imagine who would be knocking so frantically. She hurried to the door.

Cindy waited on the porch, Lorie on her hip. "Gretchen, can I come in, please?" she asked in a trembling voice. Lorie watched Gretchen solemnly.

"Come in! What is it?" Gretchen asked, closing the door behind her.

Lorie slid from her arms and went to find Julia and Bucky. Cindy hugged her arms, as if cold, even though the house had already become so warm that Gretchen had been about to turn on the cooler. Cindy had pulled her brown hair into a tight ponytail at the back of her head, revealing her haggard face, the sunken, red-rimmed eyes filled with desperation.

"What's happened?" Gretchen asked, and Cindy shook her head.

"It's Scott. He pushed me around and knocked me down. See," she said, her thin hand shaking. She pointed to a large, bluish-green bruise on the back of her arm. "He did that yesterday."

"Cindy! Jesus, what is going on? Why..."

"He's just gone crazy!" she threw up her hands. "He's been drinking. His brother called and said he's not so sure about finding Scott a job, like he promised. They're shutting off the phones tomorrow, because I haven't paid the bill. We're supposed to be out in two weeks and I don't know what we're going to do!"

"Oh, Cindy. I'm sorry," she said lamely. How could she fail to understand? Now that her own life seemed so dangerously close to the same fate.

Cindy lowered herself to the edge of the couch and put her head down, as if she suddenly felt dizzy. "I don't know where to go! He said he's going to hurt me again. I'm sorry I came here..."

"It's okay!" Gretchen said. "Where is Scott now?"

"At home," her voice rose hysterically. "He came toward me, to hit me, and I grabbed Lorie and ran over here."

Gretchen nodded, trying to think, when she heard a banging on the door.

"Oh, God. That's Scott," Cindy cried, rising and backing away from the sound of the pounding. "I know it is. Don't tell him I'm here. Please."

"But he must know you're here!" Gretchen protested. Her alarm grew as the banging persisted. "Why else would he be knocking like that?"

"Please. Tell him I'm not here," Cindy begged, then she dashed down the hall. Gretchen heard the bathroom door solidly close.

"Go back in the den," Gretchen commanded the children, who had come out when the pounding on the door started. She tried to sound calm. When the children saw the expression on her face, they retreated into the den.

"Jesus," Gretchen said, smoothing back her hair. "This is all I need."

"Who is it?" she called through the door, stalling for time.

"Gretchen. Lemme talk to Cindy," Scott said. From the tone of his voice, she could tell he knew Cindy was in the house.

She looked through the peephole and saw him swaying and stumbling on the porch, hands on hips, chest and shoulders rising as if he had been running.

"She doesn't want to see you, Scott," she yelled.

"I'm gonna see her," he said.

Where was Sam? What was she supposed to do?

"Just a minute, Scott," she said, and ran into the bathroom.

Cindy cowered in the bathtub, behind the curtain. "Why did you tell him I was here?" she moaned. "He's gonna kill me."

"He *knew* you were here!" Gretchen said, suddenly angry at being put in this position. She worried about her mother. Had the racket wakened her? "You're going to have to talk to him. Tell him to go away. Come on!"

Cindy grabbed Gretchen's shirt, her eyes wild. "Don't open the door! I know him. He's been in prison. He's dangerous. He'll hurt you, too."

Gretchen backed away. She heard her mother cry out in the next room. The pounding continued at the front door, and sounds of kicking.

"Sugar?" her mother called, and Gretchen went into her room.

Her mother sighed, her eyelids fluttering. Then she seemed to breathe more easily. Gretchen straightened her sheet, the pounding filling her ears.

"Mommy?" Julia entered the room. "Mommy, I'm scared." She stuck her thumb in her mouth, a gesture Gretchen hadn't seen in more than a year.

Gretchen crouched down and pulled the little girl into her arms. "I know. But everything will be all right."

"Why is Scott doing this?" Julia asked.

"Because he hurts so bad inside he doesn't know what to do except scream and hit and kick whatever's in front of him," Gretchen said. "Go back in the den with Bucky and Lorie. Make sure Bucky stays in the room with you, okay?"

She reached her hand into the top shelf of the closet and searched for a pair of brown loafers she hadn't worn in years. In one of the shoes, she found a small key.

She took the key, and with shaking fingers unlocked the gun cabinet. She removed the rifle and carried it down the hall, through the laundry room, and out the back door. Her heart racing, she cocked the lever and removed the safety latch. Silently, in bare feet, she tip-toed around the side of the house.

Scott still shuffled across the porch, banging and kicking the door, screaming, "Cindy!"

She stopped a few yards away from him and raised the rifle to her hip.

"Get out of here or I'll blow your head off," she said in a deadly voice.

He turned slowly, a smile of astonishment forming on his face. "I don't believe it," he said.

"I'll shoot you if I have to," she warned.

He took a step toward her and she held her ground.

"You won't shoot me," he laughed, his stringy brown hair falling over his eyes.

"The hell I won't. I've got a sick mother and two kids inside. I'm not letting you in my house."

He took two tentative steps toward her and she shot at the ground near his feet. He jumped back, howling.

"Bitch," he swore.

"I'm warning you. Get out of here," she said.

His eyes locked with hers. She braced the gun against her hip, ready to shoot again. His gaze unnerved her. His eyes were filled with hatred, as if he despised her.

"You think you're better than me, you stupid bitch. You ain't. I know all about you."

Her grip tightened on the rifle. Her palm felt moist and slippery. Sweat from her forehead dripped into her eye.

"You think you're so high and mighty. Drivin' those fancy cars and livin' in a big fancy house. I know your husband got laid off, just like me. I see him, home all the time now. He's no better than me, is he? And you lost your car, didn't you?" He sneered at her contemptuously. "You know what you are, lady? You're white trash. Just like me. You ain't no different, we'll see in the long run. When we're both on the streets."

Gretchen's hands shook. She heard a noise to one side of her and glanced quickly to see the garage door opening. Thank God, she thought with massive relief. She caught the glint of Sam's sports car near the driveway behind them, about to pull in. He probably hadn't seen them yet, through the trees.

She lowered the gun slightly as the car approached, expecting Scott to back down now. In one quick motion, Scott was beside her, grabbing the rifle.

"No!" she yelled, refusing to let go. The rifle went off, exploding in her hands. Scott sprinted away through her front yard toward his house.

"What the hell is going on here?" Sam came running toward her.

Limply, she held the smoking rifle. She stared into the open garage where the shot had been fired.

"Oh, no. Oh, Jesus," she cried. She dropped the gun and stumbled to the garage.

The papier-maché elephant, almost completed for Julia's birthday party, lay on its side. Its head had been completely blown off by the gunshot. Still smoking, the head had been thrown to the opposite side of the garage from the charred body. Tendrils of flames licked the strips of colored paper she had so lovingly glued on the previous evening.

"Your elephant," Sam said lamely.

She gazed mournfully at the piñata that she had worked so hard on, now a ruined, headless mess by her own hand. She spun around and stormed past Sam, then leaped into the car. She gunned the engine and slammed it into reverse. Then she tore out of the driveway without looking back, the sound of approaching sirens shrill in her ears.

Chapter Twenty Three

❦❦❦

Hours later, after driving randomly all over the valley, Gretchen pulled in front of the church where Rósa attended her support meetings. She didn't know what had drawn her to the church–perhaps because Rósa had found such solace here, perhaps because of Luís.

She didn't see anybody outside, yet the church door stood wide open, beckoning. She got out of the car and entered the building.

"Hello?" she called timidly. The alter lay ahead, lustrous in the sunlight that filtered through the stained glass windows. Tentatively, she walked down the aisle, then slid into a pew.

"God," she said under her breath. She closed her eyes and bowed her head. "Somewhere, I took a wrong turn. I'm in trouble. I need your help. I'm sorry if I strayed away from you. But it's almost seemed like you haven't been in my life, since Sam lost his job. Like we don't matter as much to you. Otherwise, how could so many bad things have happened to us?" She sighed. "I have to find a way out of this mess. My daddy always said that when things got bad I should let you show me what to do. And that's what I'm doing now. I need you to help me. I'll do anything. I'll go to church more. I'll stop thinking about..."

She heard footsteps, stopping by her pew. She looked up and stared into the silent, waiting face of Luís.

"Gretchen," he murmured.

She rose, her knees weak, and he drew her into his arms.

"I can't go back right now," she said. Without asking any questions, he led her to his car. She lay her head on his shoulder and they drove in silence.

Minutes later, they reached his apartment in Sherman Oaks. When she followed him upstairs, she felt like she had fallen into a great abyss; she had reached the bottom of her life. Luís had become the only one who could still see her, the essential her. She reached for him and saw herself in the darkness of his eyes. A refugee, like all the other shattered souls who needed his shelter.

"Hold me," she whispered, and his arms closed around her, warm and enveloping.

His lips brushed her cheek, cool and soft. His fingers pulled through the curls of her hair. After a moment, she pushed him away.

"I can't," she said.

"I know," he said sadly.

"I'm...confused right now," she said. She looked about her. His apartment was bright, simply furnished, almost stark.

"You can stay with me for a while. You will be safe here."

"Thank you. I have to...be away from Sam, from the tension. I can't go back now."

"Of course."

His hand reached behind her neck, under her hair. She gave in, closing her eyes. She inhaled the odor of his skin, like lime soap, and the woody trace of his aftershave.

"I'm so tired," she said.

"Yes, mi querída." He kissed her face. She leaned against him. It had been so long since Sam had held her. She found herself slipping, drunk on the shelter of his body. His lips that kept kissing her, as cool as mist.

She surrendered to her need, and to his. Her body took on the quality of a character in her dreams: fluid, wanton, lost in a ritual and pattern that seemed beyond question. Beyond return or control. The world outside grew smaller, her passion deep and overwhelming. She clung to him until a golden light flashed behind her eyelids. She called his name, and her body rejoiced in his with aching waves of pleasure.

"Stay with me," he said in the morning. They had made love long into the night. She pulled the tangled sheet up to cover her breast.

"I can't," she said, then groaned. "What have I done?"

He pulled her into his arms and stroked her cheek. "You had to stop for a while. You had to leave so you could see the problems better, and maybe the solutions."

"I don't see any solutions."

"I love you," he said.

"I love you, too," she said, and meant it. "But I have to go back and face my life. Even if I don't want to."

"I know," he said, then chided her. "I'm just a Band-Aid."

She raised her head and kissed him softly on the cheek. His arms tightened around her. "You're not a Band-Aid. You're my lover. But I have to go back to my family."

"Your children and your mother."

"Yes," she said, the weight returning. "All the people who need me."

"And your husband?"

She stared at the ceiling. "My husband. I have to try to reach him, one more time. Do you understand?"

"Yes," he said. "And I'll be here waiting for you, if it's too late."

"I'm glad," she said. "But I can't promise you anything."

"No one ever can. Are you sorry, Gretchen?"

"No," she said honestly. "Maybe I should be. But I'm not. I used to have scorn for women who cheated on their husbands. But now I can see that life isn't so simple. Or relationships, either."

"No, they're not," he said. "I found myself more and more attracted to you over the last few months. I knew you were married–still, I couldn't help myself. Love doesn't always play by the rules–it just happens sometimes. Gretchen," he sighed, burying his face in her hair. "You're so special in your trust, your innocence, your kindness to Rósa."

Gretchen basked in his words, and realized with a pang that Sam used to speak well of her, so long ago. "The way I feel about you has kept me going these past months," she told him.

He kissed her, and she savored the last moments before she left him.

❊ ❊ ❊

"Sam? I'm home." She walked uncertainly into the house. Yet, she felt renewed, energized, as if she had been away for a long time.

"Where have you been?"

Sam's voice came from the study; she entered the room and saw him sitting at his desk in the shadows. He rarely bothered to open the curtains lately.

"Where are the kids?" she asked, averting his question.

"They're at Terry's house. She called last night and offered to take them when I told her you had gone. Cindy called a friend to come get her. She was pretty shook up."

She slid into the chair next to him. "And my mother?"

"She's all right. Rósa came to check on her in the late afternoon, and spent the night. She's here now, in her room. You were gone all night."

"Yes," she said. She leaned over and pulled open the drapes. "I'm going to check on my mother."

She left the room without glancing back at him.

"You're here," her mother said, opening her eyes as Gretchen kissed her brow.

"Yes. I'm sorry I left you. How are you feeling?"

"Bad. I wondered where you went. I heard the shots, and all the yelling."

"I know. I'm sorry if it...disturbed you." Her mother was amazingly lucid, more alert than she'd been in days.

Carole gripped Gretchen's arm. She was so weak, she could barely move her head. "Don't make the same mistake I did. Sam's a good man. You've got to stay, and find a way to make things better. Don't do what I did. You mustn't make the same mistake."

"It's all right, Mom," Gretchen said, but her mother's words unsettled her.

She had spent so much time in the past judging her mother, condemning her. Suddenly, the similarity between her mother and herself leapt into focus with startling clarity: her mother had altered her life, and destroyed their family when she had an affair with another man. Now, she had done the same. She hadn't planned to be unfaithful; she had never even thought herself capable of such an action. Yet, the events of her life had led her to Luís.

She gazed at the frail figure in the bed with new understanding. And for herself, as well. Her mother had done the best she could. She had tried to survive, and had searched only for love and comfort. As she had done, as well.

When her mother fell asleep, Gretchen went wearily back to the study.

"You were with a man, weren't you?" Sam asked quietly.

"Yes," she said. She couldn't deny it. Years ago, they had both claimed each would know if the other had an affair. Perhaps he sensed her calmness, the trace of justification. And perhaps he could see the remnant of her emotional attachment to someone other than himself, that she carried in the high color in her cheeks and the glow in her eyes. In spite of Sam and his accusing stare.

"How could you?" he asked.

"How could *you*?" she demanded.

"What are you talking about?" he asked, visibly confused.

"I'm sorry you lost your job. I know it's been tough for you, and it's not your fault. But you turned your *back* on me these months. If I got involved with someone else, it's because you weren't there for me. When I needed you most. You betrayed *me*."

He gazed at her soberly. He had shaved, she noticed. He appeared pensive and reflective, as if he only now realized how much he had hurt her. That he had driven her to another man.

"I don't see how..."

"You treated me like it was my fault, your losing your business, not being able to find a job," she said angrily, the hurt spilling out. "I've been scared, and so worried. The bank is putting the house up for sale. I don't know what we're going to do, and you don't seem to care!"

"Gretchen, I...please. I do care. You can't imagine what it's been like for me. To have failed in everything." He raised his eyes. For the first time, she saw past his usual guard to the extent of his agony. His complete humiliation.

"My father brought me up to be a businessman. Even the years I worked for Titan Technologies I was only biding my time until I had a reason to go off on my own. I knew I couldn't fail, remember? But I did! And I've tried, damn it. I've tried to find another job."

She regarded him with compassion. He was finally opening up to her. She kept quiet, afraid he would stop.

"My father won't even speak to me until I pull myself together and succeed the way he did. Everyone...you, your mother, even the kids, seem to think I'm a loser. And every time I look at you, at my family, I can see how I've let you down. I've just wanted to hide under a rock."

"Oh, Sam..."

"I'm obsolete! Worthless. I can't get a job in my field. There is no more field! The end of the Cold War took care of that. It's a dream come true, the most exciting event of this century, but I can't find a job!"

He slumped against the back of the chair, his hand rubbing his forehead. "I don't know what to do. But I know I don't want to lose you, honey. The way you drove off yesterday...I knew you would really leave. Can we...can we try and work this out?"

She hesitated. He had hurt her badly over the months, and she had learned to live without him. Could she let go of the hurt he had caused her, and let him into her life again? Yet, she had waited for this moment for so long. She had dreamed about it, lived for it.

"Is it...this man? Do you love him?"

His question hung with the weight of a boulder. She hesitated, but he held her gaze with his eyes. "I do love him," she said softly.

His face seemed to cave in. He nodded in resignation.

"But I wouldn't have slept with him if you hadn't turned away from me," Gretchen continued angrily. "I needed comfort. But I don't want to spend my life with him. I want you. You're my husband."

His eyes brightened a little. "Gretchen..."

"I admit I liked the fact that you were successful when I married you," she went on. "But that's not why I married you. You made me laugh, and treated me with respect. A lot of men thought I was a dumb hick because of the way I talk, and because I don't have much education. But you treated me like I was just as smart as you."

"You are!"

"I know. But I come from a life that some people spit on...the military, my father being an enlisted man. Not having much class. That didn't bother you. You've always been...proud of me, never ashamed."

"Of course I'm proud of you! You're smart, and beautiful, and a wonderful mother," he said, more love in his voice than she had heard in months. Her thoughts returned to what her mother had said a few minutes ago...don't make the same mistake I did. Her father had rejected her mother in the same situation. But here was Sam, willing to start over and try again. She wanted to reach out to him. Yet, she held back.

"Sam...if we're going to make things better we're going to have to face our lives, together. We have to talk, and start making decisions. We have to stop blaming ourselves and each other. Somehow, maybe not now, we're going to make it back again. I know we will. But in the meantime, we have to face what we have to do, together. Is that possible?" She waited.

He reached for her hand. "I'll try. We can't go on like this. What do you want to talk about?"

She took a deep breath. "We're going to lose the house soon. I think we should sell off everything we don't need, and move into an apartment. You still have unemployment ...that will help, but one of us will have to get a job." She raised her eyebrows. "Any job. We need to do what we have to do, Sam."

She could see the pain beneath the surface of his face as he mulled over her words. "All right. I just..." His gaze swept over the room and outside the window to the backyard. Tears shined in his eyes. "I don't know if I can stand it...losing our home. All our things. I'm not giving up my piano," he said firmly. "Everything else I'll go along with. Okay?"

She smiled, feeling real hope for the first time in months. She had almost lost her marriage, her family. Could losing a house possibly compare to a reconciliation with Sam?

"Yes," she said. "We'll absolutely keep the piano."

Sam drew her into his arms, and she couldn't remember ever feeling so happy. She thought she recognized him again, that she had him back. The Sam that had first captured her heart, years ago. She cherished the moment, even if her happiness felt fragile, based on faith. Her children were safe and healthy, and she had made peace with her mother. Nothing else seemed to matter.

When she left the room to check on her mother, she heard Rósa in the kitchen and stopped to talk to her.

"Señora. Forgive me. I was in the hall and heard what you said to your husband about moving into an apartment. My cousin and her husband are moving. Our apartment has three bedrooms. It is small, but you would not have to pay a deposit to move in. Would you bring your family to live with me?"

"Oh, Rósa," Gretchen said. "How kind of you."

"You have been kind to me, Señora," she said, her lower lip trembling. "When my children died I thought I would die, too. But your family, your mother, have given me new life. She taught me how to care again. Now, perhaps I can help you."

Gretchen reached for Rósa's hands. "I would be honored to consider it," she said, and her life suddenly seemed rich beyond words.

Chapter Twenty Four

Gretchen woke during the night. Sam slept soundly beside her and she watched him for a moment, filled with tenderness.

Moonlight poured through the curtain of the open window, illuminating the room. The scent of jasmine tinged the air. Gretchen looked at her watch. Two o'clock. Compelled by an unexplained feeling, she rose and padded down the hall to her mother's room.

Her mother lay on her back, her hands peacefully at her side. A night light burned from the wall next to the bed, casting a yellow glow on her pale face. Gretchen approached, then stopped short. She touched Carole's hand. Cold. Almost frantically, she watched for the rise of Carole's chest, but it was still.

She sank into the chair next to the bed. "Mom," she said quietly. The grief welled in her chest, searing, catching in her throat as the tears blurred her vision like a liquid prism.

"I knew you were going to die," she said, her voice thick. "I knew from the start. I just...didn't know I would feel so alone. We didn't have enough time."

She took her mother's hand, so cold in her own. "I hope you knew that I loved you. That I forgave you. I'm glad you came back, even if you were sick. I'm glad that I got to take care of you." Tears slid from her eyes, onto her mother's arm.

"Do you know, somehow, how sad I am?" she whispered. "How much I miss you already? But it's okay. It's okay that it hurts. Because we had this special time."

After a few minutes she woke up Sam and called Rósa. Twenty minutes later, Rósa arrived.

"Should we call Dr. Byerly?" Sam asked. They sat around the kitchen table. Gretchen had slipped into a white cotton robe, and Sam wore an old nightshirt. Rósa, a blue shawl around her shoulders, sipped a cup of tea from a pot Gretchen had made.

"Wait until the morning," Rósa said. It was unusual for her to speak up with Sam present. "Give her spirit a chance to leave. A chance to go home. Wait until the morning, please."

Gretchen and Sam stared at each other. "All right," Gretchen said. "We'll wait until the morning, then."

"I will stay with her, if that is all right," Rósa said.

"Of course, Rósa," Gretchen said graciously, touched by her devotion. "Your bed is made up." Rósa needs a place in this family's grief, she thought. My mother's death is another in a string of losses to Rósa. Although, perhaps this one is different. Perhaps my mother helped to heal Rósa of all the other losses: her husband, missing and probably dead, and her children.

Rósa would be stronger, more whole. She would be able to go on. Gretchen was sure of it, and suddenly felt so much love for her mother. They had all been touched–Rósa, Sam, the children, and herself, by her mother's brief presence.

In the morning, before Dr. Byerly arrived, Gretchen took Julia into the easy chair with her and held her close.

"Julia," she said tentatively to the sleepy little girl, whose curly hair bounced in rhythm with the chair. "I want to talk to you about Grandma."

"Mommy. I didn't have any bad dreams last night." A curly lock of auburn hair fell over her forehead and she brushed it away impatiently. "I had a dream about Grandma, though. She sent down the stars to kiss me, and the moon to sprinkle me with magic dust. She looked wonderful, Mommy. Like an angel. She was young, and happy. And so beautiful. It was a happy dream, Mommy."

Gretchen's heart soared at her daughter's innocence, the sweetness of her dream. Bracing herself for Julia's reaction, she said, "Grandma died last night, sugar."

"Oh," Julia said in a small voice.

"She doesn't have any more pain. Would you like to see her?" She and Sam had discussed it and decided that seeing Carole's peaceful repose might help to diminish Julia's fears about death.

"She's asleep," Julia said when she saw her grandmother.

"She looks asleep, doesn't she?" Gretchen said. Rósa had washed Carole's body and combed her hair. She had dressed Carole in her long-sleeved, pink nightgown, with ruffles at the throat and pearly buttons. Rósa had elevated the head of the bed, and her mother reclined as if simply resting.

"Do you want to tell her goodbye?" Gretchen asked.

"Goodbye, Grandma." Gretchen's breath caught as Julia leaned over and softly kissed Carole's cheek. "I love you."

Rósa smiled through her tears. Gretchen pulled Julia into her lap. I wish I could hold this moment, Gretchen thought, and keep it close to my heart forever.

"Are we going to take Grandma to the tar pits, Mommy?"

"No," Gretchen said. "Grandma will be buried somewhere else."

Julia gazed at Carole for another moment. "We'll always have Grandma, won't we Mommy? Just like we have Dorothy in the movie. We'll have her in our brains and in all our pictures of her. Won't we, Mommy?"

"Yes," Gretchen agreed, taking her daughter's hand. "We always will."

"Mommy!" Julia exclaimed, spinning around, her gaze moving across the walls as if following a winging butterfly only she could see. "Grandma was right. I can still feel her love! Right here in this room, I can feel her love, all around me."

❆ ❆ ❆

On the afternoon before the sale of her house, Gretchen emptied spice bottles into a box in the kitchen.

"Honey!" Sam called to Gretchen from the den. "I think this is the last box."

Gretchen joined him and kneeled down to label the box with a marking pen. She wore loose black shorts, a yellow tank top and black beach sandals. She had helped Sam load boxes into the trailer attached to his car all morning. Only the boxes in the kitchen remained, and this one.

Sam gave her a brave smile. "Are we ready, then?"

"I don't want to leave," Julia said, then stuck her thumb in her mouth. Gretchen could hear Bucky's footsteps on the wood floors as he ran through the empty house.

Gretchen braced Julia by the shoulders. "I know you don't. But we have to."

"But this is where I live," Julia said stubbornly. "I don't want to go. I'm scared."

Gretchen bit her lip. The pain she felt for her children, losing their home, far surpassed her own. She kneeled and put her arm around Julia. "I know," she said. "This is hard. But your real home is wherever your family is. And aren't we lucky, that we're a family? And that Mommy and Daddy will always take care of you?"

"You mean like Lorie? She doesn't have a home, or a family anymore," Julia said soberly.

A week after Scott had tried to break into the house he had been arrested for parole violation. Cindy and Lorie had moved to Arizona, to live with her sister. Gretchen knew Julia missed Lorie terribly.

"Sort of," Gretchen answered, a pang going through her heart. "But Lorie and Cindy are a family, too. There are different kinds of families. In our family, we all love each other. And that's the most important thing."

"But will we ever have a house again?" she asked.

"Of course we will," Sam reassured her. "But not for a while."

Sam had finished loading the trailer. With the help of a neighbor, the piano had been loaded and pushed to the front. A pile of boxes hid it from view. The family got into the car and waited for him as he locked the doors of the house.

He slid into his seat, and glanced back at the trailer. "I can't believe this is all we have left," Sam said.

"We do have the stuff we put in storage," Gretchen said. "And we made more than we thought we would from the garage sale."

"I know," Sam said. "I guess it will take some time to get used to this."

"Give it time, Sam."

"Rósa will be home to let us in?" he asked Gretchen for the second time that day.

She touched his face. "Yes, Sam. She's waiting for us."

"I have to bring the key over tomorrow," he told her. He gazed at his house. "I'm going to miss this place."

"I will too," Gretchen admitted. "This is the only home Bucky had, and probably the only one Julia remembers. Right, sugar?"

Julia, sitting in the back seat, nodded. "I don't remember our other house."

"We had some good years here," Gretchen said, grief rising in her throat. Leaving the house felt like the hardest, most painful thing she had ever done.

"Goodbye, house!" Sam said, and waved.

"Goodbye, house!" Julia and Bucky echoed.

"Let's just go, Sam," Gretchen said, and he started the car. He pulled out of the driveway and down the hill, leaving Woodland Hills behind as he headed toward Pacoima.

❄ ❄ ❄

"Ay diós!" Rósa cried, running down the rickety stairs of her apartment to greet them with open arms. "I am so happy. You are here."

Cautiously, Sam opened his door. Smells of frying meat, laundry bleach, and the sickly, decaying smell of garbage floated into the car. Graffiti had been scrawled over the faces of the apartment buildings that stretched along the street like one jagged wall. Tufts of dry grass grew through the cracked sidewalk, and stray cats rubbed against a light pole near the car. The street looked old and dim to Gretchen. The buildings were shoddy, gray or beige with fading paint, and only a spattering of spindly trees broke up the endless surrounding of concrete and asphalt. Even though she had been here many times to drop off Rósa, she had barely noticed the neighborhood. She shrank into her seat, her senses overpowered.

"Let's go, gang," Sam urged cheerfully. Gretchen got out, then opened the door for Julia and Bucky.

A lanky young man appeared behind Rósa. "Hey man," he said to Sam. "Welcome to the barrio."

"This is my nephew, Ramón," Rósa explained. "He lives in the building next door."

"Thanks," Sam said awkwardly. "Well, here we are. In the barrio. I guess we'd better unload."

"I'll help you, man," Ramón offered, leaping off the curb to the back of the trailer.

"I'd appreciate that," Sam said, as Gretchen and the kids followed Rósa up to the apartment. "I've got a piano in there."

Ramón gave Sam a thumbs up sign. "You grab one end, I'll grab the other. I've got a dolly, if that will help."

As Gretchen stepped into her new home, the first thing she noticed was the crucifix on the wall, and the sound of Ramón's distinct offer from below.

"I'm leavin' town, man. You like to swap this car for my ice cream truck?"

Chapter Twenty Five

Six months later, Gretchen stood in the tiny kitchen of Rósa's apartment, mixing her papier-maché paste in a pottery bowl. Today, she thought, I will make a little zebra. I will make my frame out of a balloon and chicken wire, and use broom bristles for the tail. When it dries, I can paint stripes with black paint.

Sam played the piano in the living room. The piano took up almost the entire room. She recognized the pure, joyous tones of Mozart's twenty-first symphony. Soon, the children would be out of school, and Sam would drive his ice cream truck along the streets of Pacoima. Rósa was out today, cleaning a house. Tomorrow she would clean, and Rósa would watch Bucky and pick up Julia from kindergarten.

Life is better, now that the trouble is behind us. We have lost our money, and our old way of life. But we are a family again, with Rósa included. I don't mind cleaning houses–I can work alone, with no one to bother me. And Sam has a following of children that keeps him smiling long after he has brought home the truck. If life doesn't get any better than this for a long time, we will survive.

She found a brush in her craft cupboard, under the pantry, and lay it on Rósa's green Formica table with her other supplies. She added more starch to the bowl of paste and stepped over to the piano to listen, stirring her mixture.

"Beautiful," she said when he had finished. "You used to play those heavy, mournful pieces."

"That's because I'm *light as a bird*!" he said, rising to spin her around.

"Sam!" she laughed, clutching the bowl of paste. A drop spilled onto one of the chipped piano keys.

"Are you happy, honey?" he asked, devotion in his blue eyes. "Do you ever think of...?"

She saw the uncertainty, the fear, and rushed to reassure him. "Only to hope that he is well, and happy," she said truthfully. She had seen Luís once since the night they had spent together. He had embraced her, then let her go. He had known, even in his love for her, that she needed to be with her husband. That she had found a second chance.

"And you?" she asked. "Are you happy, Sam?"

"I have the best wife and kids that a man could ask for. So what if I'm not making bombs anymore, or driving a new car? There are other good things in life. I kind of like my ice cream truck, and the kids on the streets. Life is simple now. I have more time to play with Julia and Bucky, and my piano."

"All the kids adore you. Your own and the ones in the neighborhood. Here, let me try something," she said. She went to the table, and brought back the little brush. With careful strokes, she blended the spilled paste into the piano key.

"Pretty good," she declared with satisfaction. "Almost like new again."

Sam stared at the key, his face assuming a strange expression. "My God, Gretchen," he exclaimed finally. "It completely covers up the chip, and the brown spot. It almost looks like..."

"Sam! What is it?"

Opened-mouthed, he continued to look at the piano key, as if spellbound. Then he leaped across the room, dove into a closet, and returned with a screwdriver. Furiously, he began taking the piano apart, his forehead beading with sweat. Triumphantly, he held up the key that Gretchen had painted with her papier-maché paste. He bounded to the door, and grabbed the keys to his ice cream truck from a hook on the wall.

"Gretchen!" he yelled. "I have to GO TO THE DENTIST!!"

❄ ❄ ❄

The light had begun to dim in the apartment when Gretchen heard Sam's key in the lock. Rósa had returned two hours earlier, and taken the children with her to the laundromat.

"Sam?" she asked anxiously. The way he had run out of the apartment like a maniac had kept her wondering all day. Did he have another toothache? If so, why had he seemed so excited?

"Gretchen!" Sam strode into the little living room, carrying a bouquet of yellow roses.

"Sam?" Gretchen dropped her dishtowel. "Are you crazy? We can't afford–"

"Gretchen, you're a genius!" he said joyfully, proudly presenting her with the flowers.

"I am?" She took the flowers in her arms, and couldn't resist burying her nose into the buds; the sweet perfume and refrigerator coolness filled her nostrils.

"What has happened?" she asked.

He pulled a rickety chair from the table for her, guiding her into the seat while sitting down himself. "Honey, it's a miracle. I wish I had thought of it years ago. Dr. Mosier. The piano keys–"

"Sam, what are you talking about?" Gretchen laughed, inhaling again from the fragrant roses.

"Gretchen, don't you understand? It's over. I'm onto something big that will take us out of here and be a contribution at the same time. Something we can feel good about."

Gretchen shook her head. "Sam? Slow down, please."

He took a deep breath. He seemed so agitated, she thought he would fly out of the chair. "Do you remember this morning, when your papier-maché paste covered the chip in that ivory piano key so well? It suddenly came to me. Everything. The elephants in Africa you've been so worried about. Those horrible plastic keys that are used to replace damaged ivory piano keys."

"Yes?" Gretchen urged him to continue.

"I met with Dr. Mosier. He says we can do it, without a doubt. Gretchen. We can develop a dental bonding material to repair ivory piano keys. A synthetic ivory. Dr. Mosier says he can make a material that would be almost indistinguishable from ivory. Can you imagine?" His eyes blazed with excitement.

Gretchen dropped the roses on the table. "Oh, Sam. It sounds wonderful. Do you really think it will work?"

He leaned toward her and grasped her hand. "Honey. Dr. Mosier and I spent the afternoon calling markets. Piano dealers. Piano repair companies and jewelry importers. The response we got was incredible, Gretchen. Everyone we talked to asked us to send them information on our product." He sprang up from the chair, knocking it over. "We have a new business! We're going to make it, Gretchen!"

❄ ❄ ❄

Three months later, Gretchen strode into the new office followed by Julia and Bucky. "Well, here you all are!" Dr. Mosier exclaimed. "What a nice surprise."

Gretchen grinned, looking smart in her new forest-green pants and matching jacket, with a jeweled elephant pin on the lapel. Her black-and-white cowboy boots, with silver tips on the toes, clicked on the entryway until she stepped onto the new, silver carpet.

Dr. Mosier and Sam had moved in two weeks ago. Dr. Mosier's old office had been sufficient for a while, but now they needed more room. The place exuded the early chaos of a new business: unpacked boxes still on the floor, employees bustling about, eager to please, and desks littered with papers.

"Happy birthday," Dr. Mosier said. A small man, he reached up to kiss Gretchen on the cheek. "Did something arrive for you today?" he asked mischievously.

"I got the flowers, Ron," Gretchen said with a satisfied glow. "I stopped by to thank the boy, personally."

"He's at his new dentist," Dr. Mosier said, then seeing her downcast face, added, "It's just a cleaning, Gretchen. Nothing major. He should be back soon."

Relieved, she said, "Sam says the business is going pretty well."

"Pretty well?" He flashed his teeth, the wide, unabashed smile of a dentist. "Come here, let me show you something. You too, kids."

He grabbed Bucky, who seemed too surprised to protest, and carried him into the next room. Gretchen and Julia followed.

Long tables along the back of the room were stacked with blocks of the off-white, chalky substance. Four young men worked quickly to pack the material in boxes, while shuffling through reams of paperwork.

"Are you a Republican?" one of the men asked, eying her pin.

"No!" she said, slightly startled.

"See this?" Ron said, gesturing toward the blocks. "We've decided to call it Ivoron. Did Sam tell you?"

She nodded.

"This shipment will be sent out of here by the end of the week. We just hired another technician to help with production, and two more chemists from UCLA for research and development, so we can keep up with the demand."

"Wow," Gretchen said. "Where...where will most of it go?"

"Overseas, mostly, and to piano repair shops. Keys made from this substance are identical to ivory piano keys. Most of the big orders have been coming from jewelers, and ivory dealers."

"Ivory dealers?" Gretchen fingered the pin on her lapel.

Dr. Mosier turned toward her. An older man, he had a fatherly gentleness that made her feel safe. "We're hopeful that elephant ivory will be a thing of the past. Once people see that our product is identical in every way to ivory, and can be used for the same purposes, there won't be any need to slaughter elephants."

Her expression froze, then she looked quickly about for her children.

"Is something wrong?" Dr. Mosier asked.

She drew Bucky and Julia to her side and kneeled down between them.

She gazed up at him calmly, her eyes as clear as jade. "No, Ron. Nothing is wrong. In my world, everything is finally perfect."

❄ ❄ ❄

"Gretchen!" Sam approached her car in the parking lot, just as she turned the key.

She stepped out of the car. Striking in his charcoal-gray pants and blue sports shirt, his blue eyes teased her as he stepped close.

"Anything interesting happen today?"

"Somebody sent me some flowers for my birthday," she said coyly.

"Should I be jealous?"

She put her arms around his neck. His shoulders had become broader since he had started working out again. She turned her head to see Julia pointing at them from the front seat of her new station wagon, trying to arouse the interest of her brother.

"You don't ever have to be jealous," she whispered in his ear. "I love you." The rubber tip of his gum stimulator, sticking out of his shirt pocket, caught on her elephant pin.

"Sorry," he said sheepishly, returning it to his pocket. "And what about your present?"

Her eyes lit up. "You replaced the ivory handles of my .38 with Ivoron! I love it."

"I thought you would," he said, kissing her.

"It looks like you and Ron are getting settled," she said.

"Do you like the place? I thought it was such a big office at first, but now I see we needed the room. And the way sales are going, we'll be able to pay Ron back soon enough for assuming the costs–"

"I'm proud of you, Sam. From the day I met you, I knew you could succeed at something important."

He held her for a moment. "Hey! Guess what? I got a letter from Entrepreneur magazine today."

"Yes?"

"They're considering us for their Clean and Green Fifty environmental award!"

"Sam," she squealed. "That's wonderful!"

A blast from the horn interrupted their embrace. Bucky had climbed into the front seat, and had turned on the lights as well.

"I'd better get back to the apartment," Gretchen said. She opened the car door and nudged Bucky into the rear seat. "I promised Rósa I'd take her shopping for some new dresses."

"Okay. Don't forget I'm coming home early today."

She gave him a blank look.

He put his hands on his hips and laughed at her. "Have you actually forgotten? I can't believe it. We're going to go house hunting!"

Biographical Note

Katie Carothers was born and raised in Altadena, California. She received her BSc degree in Education from the University of Southern Illinois, and a BSc degree in Computer Science from Central State University of Oklahoma. Ms. Carothers lives in Los Angeles with her husband and two children.